I0635770

CHASING STARS

MARTHA TJARKS

Chasing Stars
© 2020 by Martha Tjarks
Published by Austin Brothers Publishing

ISBN—978-1-7333130-8-7

Chasing Stars is a work of fiction. Names, characters, places, and incidents are products of the author's imagination or are used fictitiously. Any resemblance to actual events, places, or persons, living or dead, is coincidental, unintentional, or if real, to provide a sense of authenticity and used fictitiously

Printed in the United States

Episodes

Episode 1

The space programs have been in full swing for about ten years now but only recently have negotiations taken place between Humans and Sanarians. The space program is still working on finishing the three lead spaceships that will explore the space between Earth and Sarani (Sar-a-nigh) and beyond. They discovered Earth before their program was up and running, but now they are catching up quickly. So far, there have only been a few contained meetings, and they have been held at the massive 20 building complex known as Earth Central. It is an impressive area because it is Earth's interstellar position to the universe. An energy shield surrounds it like a dome, so only humans travel beyond the dome.

In addition to these rather informal meetings, there have been numerous broadcast video conversations between the two planets. The two populations have been able to learn a lot about each other safely this way. That is how Earth Central got its name. The space program on Sarani is operated from a campus of many buildings called Sarani Central in their language. On their first visit, the Sanarians (Sa-nar-ee-N) shared their universal translator technology that breaks all language barriers. Earth Central mass-produced them rather quickly in the first year. Earth Central does an excellent job of making public presentations out of everything they learn and everything they share about humankind so that most of the public is aware of everything going on.

Today the news teams are out at the front entrance covering the group of 50 protesters that prefer Sanarians not set foot on the planet. The majority of citizens are excited about the possibilities that an era of space exploration will bring. This isn't a story about space exploration; it's a story about two planets trying to figure out how to get along, and two unique citizens destined to be pitted against each other.

Today's protest isn't unique, it's a little larger than usual, and it's a slow news day, hence the smattering of press present. There is another group about to get a bit more serious about insisting humanity not mix with Sanarians, and today they start their campaign.

It's a mild April afternoon in Texas. The wind is light; it's around 73 degrees and likely to rain tomorrow.

In front of one of the retail buildings on the left of the campus, a white van is parked. It is a store that sells uniforms to the officers who are training to be astronauts on the giant floating cities that make up the first three space ships about to go into service. They are built for science and defense, not offense, and some think its a bad idea. The white van has been sitting there all night, with no occupants. Anyone who might be curious simply assumed it was a reporter's equipment truck. Even security ignored it.

Then in a flash, the van erupted in a massive explosion and wiped out half the clothing store. A few reporters and protesters were close enough to get thrown to the ground by the blast, but it missed the main group. Everyone still standing ran away.

The story of this blatant terrorist attack dominated the news for the next week. Though there are injuries, only eight were killed, and they were workers in the store. The news media began speculation that one of the protest groups were behind the attack, but it's all speculation.

A six-foot-tall college-age female with brown hair steps into the living room of a modest ranch house owned by her parents. Her name is Tygeria (ta-gear-ra), but that's a little unique, so she usually goes by Tyger, less unique, but it works. Sanarians don't exist outside of Earth central, but she does, because she was born here. She acts human and mostly wishes she were. It would be more comfortable than feeling like she's hiding.

"I think I'm going to join Earth Central. Maybe I can help. Maybe if I'm part of the space program, I can learn more about my father's planet." Tygeria says.

"I don't know that it would be safe," Pa warns. Pa is 5 foot 9 and 180 pounds of cowboy. He grew up in the south on a ranch that raised cows. His brown hair and green eyes look nice when he wears his plaid shirt tucked into his dark blue jeans.

"I think I can handle myself," Tygeria replies.

"Your clever, quick, and you've got a trusting heart, that is not what I'm worried about," Pa says as he placed bowls on the table, "The problem is your too nice. Even to those who would harm you."

"Well, why would anyone harm me, if I'm nice?" Tygeria said. "After all, the space program has been growing by leaps and bounds for years now. We're in the 22nd century, and we have finally stopped fighting each other and started fighting over space dominance. The Earth Central Program is seeking out other life. I should almost just go and say 'Hi, I hear you've been looking for me.'"

"They are looking for other people," Pa explained, "and other worlds and greater understanding. Your mother was human, a friend of ours. That's why we know your Sanarian name. You were born here on Earth; you are different because your half Sanarian but your not exactly what they are looking for. You would only make them nervous because you're different in the things you do, not the way you look. We are grateful you don't look different, so you can just blend right in, and people will leave you alone."

Pa sat down at the table, "I'm so proud of you and your kind heart. Last week you stopped a runaway semi, froze out two house fires…"

"Three actually," Tygeria corrects him.

"Three house fires," he continues, "and found the lost hikers within an hour in that huge national park. That's a pretty good impact on doing good for the world. You did all that from the shadows hiding under that cloak. The news is calling you the Angel of Worth. Is that not enough? Helping with natural disasters and stopping accidents. You should be proud of that. Do you need more?"

"Are you afraid?" Tygeria askes. "Do you worry if I join a starship I will find home and leave you guys. You're my family, I would never do that," Tygeria replied, serving herself a scoop of the scrambled eggs.

Ma walks in and sits at the table. Ma and Pa met in high school and have been together since. She is an outdoor girl, but she's a little more of the city type. Despite that, she has always loved horses, so they were a good match to fall in love with and run a ranch. She handles the business end of things while Pa handles the animals. Ma is 5 foot 5 and always in charge. She keeps her blond hair long tied up in a ponytail. She is wearing a short sleeve button up blouse and blue jeans. Her typical look. Thin rimmed glasses rest on her nose, and the cell phone is always in the pocket.

"You would not find home; this is home; you're half-human; after all, I knew your mother since she was a kid, and I promised her when she died that I would keep you safe," Ma says.

Tygeria's birth mother died when Tygeria was only two years old. These guys where her godparents and have raised her ever since. They knew Tygeria's mother for a long time, but they only knew her dad for a short time. He was only around for about five years. When her mom died, these two were with her, and she told them Tygeria was only half-human. The other half is Sanarian, people from another planet. Her dad's ship made an emergency landing, unnoticed. He thought he was stranded forever, so he blended in and fell in love and started a family. Then one of his people came to rescue him. They took him by force and messed it all up. Consequently, Tygeria is half Sanarian and half Human and being raised by her foster parents.

"You two will always be my parents, but if I can do more and see more, I should," Tygeria said. "My birth father might be alive, after all. The space program will inevitably find land and make contact with Sarani. I kinda think I should be there when they do,"

"You will also be going from the angel in the shadows that helps with accidents to someone stopping people from doing harm. That makes enemies. Those are the people that will target you and hurt you. And you, sweetheart, you are too afraid of hurting anyone and will let them do you harm. You're not invincible or bulletproof. I think you should just keep helping the city of Worth. Go get a normal job as a salesman or something now that you have graduated from college. You can take a year and find yourself before you march off to Earth Central. You won't be able just to march up and join the security team so easily with no background in security, especially as a female."

"So I'll practice fighting, and maybe in the meantime, they will let me, average plain Jane, help with the observation end of security." Tygeria grinned and proceeded to eat her eggs.

"You can be anything you want, dear Tyger," Ma assured. "Just do it carefully and take your time. There's nothing you have to do today but to take care of the outer fence that fell. You were out late last night did you get enough sleep?"

"Yeah," Tygeria said, "thankfully, last night, things were kinda quiet."

Tyger's family has a ranch home in Texas. They raise and board horses, but they currently only have a few. In the past, they had many more, but they dialed back when they took early retirement. Tygeria is dressed in her blue jeans and a long flowing print top. She favors tunics since she is six feet tall. She has medium length brown hair that she ties back when she's working.

It's a large house that has been in the family for two generations. The walls are paneled with wood and a lot of open deck space wrapping around the back facing a swimming pool. Pa put solar power on the roof a while back, and it's tapped into well water, so there are very few bills. There is a large fireplace on the west side and two little ones that tap into the big brick chimney as it passes through the upstairs level. They joke that all the heat is only on one side of the house, but it's Texas, and there's not much of a winter. On the downstairs level, it's the focal point of the open deck, but the upstairs extends over it a bit, making the deck almost feel like a room. The family spends most of their time there except during the hot months. Tyger loves the smell of a good campfire, so they almost always have a small fire smoldering in the outdoor fireplace, wafting the rich aroma of hickory or pecan wood across the property.

Tyger stepped down off of the back deck and through the fence of the first horse paddock. There are three fenced areas and one large barn. Tyger walked the fence line of the third paddock over to an area that needs repair. A recent storm knocked two sections down, mostly because they were old wood. Tyger puts her hand on one of the fallen massive crossbeams, and it subtly starts to glow with a blue light spreading out like liquid, filling the post until the whole wood beam has a blue light on it. This lets her pick it up with ease. Tyger has to worry about the size of it, but for her, it is now weightless. She sets it aside on the ground and, in the same way, supports all the pieces from the two sections. There is just the snapped post sticking out of the ground that needs to be pulled.

Pa has walked over with his toolbox and sets it down as she ponders the last piece. "Well, looks like we can reuse most of it," he says.

Pa has had this property in his family for two generations. He built his own house on the opposite end of his father's house. None of his relatives are alive anymore, but then Ma and Pa are both in their sixties. They knew her mother. Clearly, she was human, but Tygeria's biological father was a traveler, an explorer. A scout if you will. They usually try to stay hidden and don't interact with a new planet, but he was hurt. He met Tygeria's mother and kept coming back to her.

Then something happened, and he couldn't come anymore. Pa assumed he lost his ship somehow, so he and Ma took care of them. Pa's closet is full of flannel shirts, jean jackets, and baseball caps. Boots and blue jeans are his go to as well, but then what else can you do tending horses all day. Pa sorts through his tools, lifts his hat to scratch his short curly black hair, and grabs a crowbar.

Tygeria grabs one of the two main posts that are still sticking out of the ground, half-broken, and fills the post with energy and yanks it up, concrete and all. Then she flings it with ease about five feet to her right. She peaks into the hole to make sure she got all the concrete. She definitely needs to replace both if there is any wood left.

"There should still be about ten posts that we haven't touched yet sitting in the back corner of the barn," Pa sayd, "I will bring them while you finish pulling up that other broken piece. Do you think we need anything else out of the barn?"

"Just some more wire, I suppose, I only brought enough for one I didn't realize two were broken."

Tygeria starts working on pulling up the other post as Pa walks in the direction of the barn.

Ten minutes later, he pulls up in a golf cart with two fresh posts sitting in the wagon trailing behind. "I brought you some gloves. It would be a shame to get hurt on a project so small as this," Pa says,

"Oh good, thank you."

She grabs one of the beams out of the back of the wagon, takes it over, and rams it in the ground in the previous hole but even further down. As she does this, she infuses it with energy, and it passes through the dirt smoothly, almost like the soil's not there. When she releases, she takes all of her energy out of the object; the post, in this case, turns solid again, but it is fused with enough of the dirt and leftover concrete To stay put very securely anchored in place.

"So are you gonna join security or something else? I know your thinking security because you're used to thinking of protecting people," Pa says.

"Well, I was just thinking, I'm not gonna walk right into an ambassadorship or anything," Tygeria answers. "On the other hand, it feels like every night I go on patrol, that security force, the police, is one of the main entities I'm hiding from."

"What are you trying to do?" Pa asks.

"We've talked about this," Tygeria says.

"I know, say it again," Pa says.

"This is one of those lessons, fine. I need people to be hopeful and not automatically afraid of aliens just because they can do different things," responded Tygeria.

"I think that would take some time and would be a very important lesson for the security team at Earth Central. They need that perspective most of all for this space program to really work. Agreed?" Pa says. "And I think you would be a great person, maybe the only person that can teach them that."

"Why would they listen to me?" Tygeria asks. "This is how to treat the weirdos as told by the most public weirdo."

"That's why you don't tell them," Pa smiles, "You make them ask, you show that you've got it figured out and make them want to emulate that. No fear, just an open-minded approach to learning about others. You keep doing what you're doing, helping as many people as you can figure out a way to help. Just..be careful and don't bite off more than you can handle. Trying a bunch of stuff you can't actually help with and failing at it miserably will have the opposite effect of what you're trying to do. Which is why I think your Ma and I just want you to take your time and keep doing your patrols for now. And maybe nothing with guns, you're not bulletproof."

"OK," Tygeria grins at Pa, "Thanks. Always there to help me figure it out." She hugs him and starts cleaning up the tools.

A few hours pass, and now Tygeria pulls up in front of Debbie's house in her pickup truck and parked on the street. The weather is beautiful. It rained yesterday, and she can still smell some of the wet on the grass and trees. It's just perfect, not too hot, not too cold. A great day to be outside. That'll change soon as summer is right around the corner and the good old Texas heat. But right now, it's pleasant, and the fresh air put a little extra bit of a spring in her step as she walks up the sidewalk to the front porch and rings the bell.

She stands there, admiring Debbie's latest bloom of irises in her front garden right beside a beautiful covered porch.

"Hey sweet girl, what you been up to lately?" Debbie says. They were roommates all through college, and now that they have graduated, Debbie stays at her Aunt's house on the edge of downtown. Her Aunt travels for work and is only home one week a month, Debbie gets to watch the place for her. Better than being stuck in an apartment.

Debbie and Tyger have been friends for quite a while. It's always good to see her. She's one of the few people who know who Tyger is, that she's not from this planet entirely. She does know that Tygeria sneaks out in the middle of the night, gliding around the city helping anyone she can and often helps her

with it. She's one of the few friends Tyger has that is
entirely safe.

Debbie is 5'9 and skinny with long blond hair that
almost reaches her waist. She wears blue jeans most
of the time and rotates through a favorite collection
of pastel button-up shirts. Debbie has been a strict
vegetarian since high school, spurred by her desire to
become a vet. Five days a week, she spends the morn-
ings at a shared vet practice. Off by 4 pm, she's always
ready in the evenings when Tygeria is ready to go out
and patrol after dark. Sometimes Tygeria just calls
when she gets started, and most of the time, Tygeria
goes over and hangs out between 4 and darkness before she gets started.

Debbie has also been writing a vet blog since her
college days. Since Tygeria went to college with her
and knows this, she asks Debbie to start writing about
her anonymously.

"You trying to be some superhero, like in the com-
ic books?" Debbie asks.

"I just want to get ahead of the fear. People being
afraid of an alien who is obviously able to different
things they can't understand, my folks are so scared
of what afraid people will do to me if they figure me
out," Tygeria explains. "There are too many people
afraid of too many unknowns. All I wanna do is help."

"I know you do," Debbie says, "You're one of those people that can't stand idly by and watch someone else get hurt."

"I have decided that the best thing to fight fear is knowledge," Tygeria proclaims. "Still leave my anonymity but tell them everything else. Tell them I'm not an invader. When I help as much as I can, and people are mad that I couldn't get to their loved one, or they wanted some miracle that no one could have helped with, you can explain that and help them understand that all effort is being made. Just don't put yourself at risk, either."

"Yeah, that's perfect. I will write the first based off of whatever we find for you to help with this week, and we will look at them together before I publish," Debbie says. "The news doesn't seem to be doing you any favors. Some of the stuff you helped with last month just got credited to the police instead."

"That's fine, the police are good, and no one's looking for me," Tygeria says.

"But if you want some press out there to prepare everyone not to be afraid of the Sanarians that Earth Central keeps talking too, you need to get more of that goodwill publicity under your own name, right," Debbie points out.

"Well, I started looking at getting a job," Tygeria replies.

"At Central?" Debbie asks.

"Of course," Tygeria replies.

"What kind of position do you think you can get?" Debbie asks, grabbing a cup of coffee and leaning against the kitchen counter.

"That's where I'm stuck for now, but I'd rather leave that pondering for another day. I've been mending fences all day, and the sun is going down soon." Tyger says.

"Your point is?" Debbie almost laughs; she has a terrible poker face.

"I'm restless and bored," Tygeria insists.

"OK, OK." Debbie laughs. She turns around the laptop on the kitchen counter to face her and starts typing. "Let's see what we've got to play with. I want to get started with the blog as soon as possible; not missing a moment."

"Low profile, invisible even," Tygeria says. "No spotlight right at me. That are too many people out there who would be either afraid of me or curious, and I'm not a lab rat."

"I know, I know. And true, there are more and more sightings of spaceships and disappearances. Sure, some people are afraid, but you said it yourself, Central is proof that there are also some people looking at interstellar relations the right way. Here's my point. You said the main reason you sneak around every night in the dark and save people is so that people might also like aliens and see them as potential helpers too. I think the fear is escalating, but if I start giving you a lot of good press and build you up as a superhero or something like in the movies, it might help your cause for creating a good strong image. Now I don't necessarily agree that this strong image of yours should be anonymous, I know why you worry about that, so just like a superhero, we only get you a look and an image, so no one tracks you down at your home or anything."

"Thank you, that's actually a good thought, and it probably would help a lot. Tell you what. Do a few and then show me what your thinking, and I bet we can get something that works that I'm comfortable with," Tyger smiles.

"But what about tonight," Debbie says, "I know, I know. Thankfully watching social media means even the start of trouble is public quickly, so I bet we can get better at getting there to stop something instead of just hearing about it after it happens and helping clean up. I mean, you're great with putting out fires with that touch and freeze thing you do. No fires tonight, though. I have a cargo train derailed three hours ago about 100 miles from here."

"Did the conductor get out, OK?" Tygeria asks.

"Looks like," Debbie says, "but you fill those train cars with that bioenergy you've got and pick them right up in the air and get them back on the tracks."

"Not looking to get in the habit of cleaning up messes, I think we should focus on saving lives," Tyger says.

"True," Debbie says as she keeps scrolling, "maybe I can find a cat in a tree?"

"Oh, hush, ha-ha," Tyger says as she grabs a glass from Debbie's cupboard and fills it with water from the sink. "As you say so far, it's a dull quiet night."

"Kinda," Debbie smiles. "Wait a minute; here we go, there's a bank robbery alarm over on 7th street."

"As much as I'd like to handle that, I'm not bullet-proof," Tygeria says, "maybe I can sneak up on them and dust their guns before they see me, but that only works if there are three or fewer. I can, what are we calling it, shift that short distance fast move that can pop me from one end of the room to another. If there are a lot of them, the fourth or fifth person would see me coming and grab me or shoot me."

"Come on, you go change into your cloak and glide over there, I'll meet you; just look for my truck," Debbie says, grabbing her keys.

Four bank robbers are hooking their truck up to an outdoor ATM. It's too late for the bank to be open, but the ATM will be full at this hour. Someone across the street saw them messing with chains and hooks and called it in. Somehow Tygeria gets there before the police, just in time to see them pull away, dragging the machine out of the wall. They stop the truck and run back to load up their prize, but it is taking a minute because it's so heavy.

The men left the truck running and are scrambling to unhook the chains and see if they can take just the money out yet, but they can't. Tygeria lands, slamming down right into the back of their truck.

"I don't think that's yours," Tygeria says to the startled group.

"Where'd you come from?" one robber says.

"What are you gonna do about it?" another robber says.

Tygeria lets her energy concentrate and feels it flow from her center down her arm to her fingertips. She works it through her fingers like she was pulling thread until enough concentrates that it starts binding to itself, and a ball of bright blue energy floats in the center of her hand. She expands her hand, and now she has an energy sphere the size of a bowling ball but weightless. It is floating in front of her, not attached to her hand, and yet somehow mentally, it is. Like she is tossing a softball, she flings it toward the ATM, and suddenly the entire machine is encased in ice. The four men jump back. Then she freezes their truck the same way. One pulls out a gun, so Tygeria shoots up into the night sky and leaves, spotting the red and blue flashing police lights approaching from two blocks away.

Tygeria sees Debbie's truck four blocks to the East, so she lands in the dark ally and changes outfits. Then she steps out and flags Debbie down as she was about to rush past trying to catch up to the action.

"Don't get too close to that mess; they've got guns," Tygeria says, hopping in the truck. "They pulled the ATM out of the wall with their truck. So while they were out of the truck, I froze the ATM and the truck, so they can't leave. "

"That should work since a witness already called it in, I'm sure the police will round up all four of the guys," Debbie says. "Let's get back on patrol before more police swarm this section."

Debbie drives around to the other end of downtown by the cultural district. Everything is quiet over there, so she parks at the city park and pulls out her laptop to check for any new reports. Tygeria decides to glide through the streets high enough to not be at all visible, well over the tops of the buildings, but low enough to see people and cars. They patrol for several more hours. Tygeria keeps her cell phone in a pouch on her uniform with a Bluetooth headset in her ear.

This way, she and Debbie can call each other, and Tygeria can talk even while up in the air patrolling.

Debbie has amassed a prime collection of web sites and one police scanner that she uses to try to get a lead on trouble soon enough for Tygeria to make a difference. The sad truth is most events just happen in an instant, and there is nothing police or paramedics or heroes in cloaks can do but to go help clean up after. Tygeria promised Pa that she'd leave the clean up for the police and paramedics, so she doesn't get herself in "real" trouble. After several hours it is clear the city has gone to sleep, so they meet back at Debbie's house.

So how much can that outfit of yours protect you from? Is it fireproof?" Debbie asks.

"I don't know; got a candle?" Tygeria says.

Tygeria uses a portion of this bioenergy to create energy threads; there is a memory to it. With a thought, the outfit she put on that morning changes to her uniform and can just as smoothly change back. While it is quick, it is not instant. The transformation flows down, cascading from top to bottom. This lets her change quickly and hide in plain sight to keep disguised as the city angel.

Debbie helped her with the design of the uniform. It is a blue, white, and silver pantsuit with a long tunic top and a cloak that sweeps off to the left. She can completely hide under the cloak hood when needed to protect herself from the elements.

"Come here, let's try this," Debbie says, pulling a candle and box of matches out of the kitchen drawer and setting them on the counter. Tygeria switched into uniform and pulled the corner of her cloak up onto the table.

"Hold it steady, and we will see how long it takes to catch fire," Debbie says, lighting the candle. They keep the material that feels slick like silk, but it has a little more weight to it. They hold it over the candle for 20 minutes, and nothing even marks the fabric. So Tygeria gets bold and grabs the cloth and then puts her hand over the flame.

"Ha, that works well. I kinda feel the heat from the fire, but I also feel cold. It's like I'm automatically chilling the cloak in reaction to the heat," Tygeria says.

"Can you do that, can you make your uniform hot or cold?" Debbie asks.

"Well, I can make the raw energy, the sphere, into three states. It can cause an object inside it to turn to fire, ice, or dust. Apparently, since the uniform is made from similar energy, it can take on that effect a bit too. It's reactive, I've noticed I stay pretty warm when flying through the cold wind. That will always be a subconscious effect.

"Well, I'll stop trying to scuff up your outfit," Debbie says, blowing out the candle. "This makes you even more suited to help with fires, but what else can you handle because we got no fires on the reports tonight."

"I can find missing people sometimes," Tygeria points out.

"Oh yeah, you found those hikers last week and took them back to the ranger station." Debbie says, "I never did ask, did you walk them back, or did you pick them up and glide them down to the Ranger station?"

"Well, there were no news cameras there, and it would have been such a long walk." Tygeria says, "I energized a tree, asked the husband to stay there, and picked the wife up by the waist, and flew her down. Then I could tell quickly where that energized tree was, even though it was in the middle of a 250-acre state park. I went back to it and grabbed the husband and took him to the Ranger station. I dropped him off a little further away to not land on top of the crowd that had developed for search and rescue. They were swarming the poor wife, who wasn't sure what to say at that point. Once the husband's feet were on the ground, he started running toward his wife, so I took off as quickly as possible before anyone could whip out their phone and start taking pictures. I never knew what kind of reaction they had to gliding because I didn't stick around to say what did you think of the trip."

"I've checked the Angel sites. There are no new pictures from that, so your good," Debbie says. "Someone will interview them and write it up. It might just take a few more days for me to find. That one just happened last week."

"I wish they wouldn't call me Angel; I'm not," Tygeria says.

"It's referring to a guardian angel, and they don't know what else to call you. At least that is positive branding," Debbie laughs. "This blog we've been talking about, would you like me to put your real name out there?"

"Yes, just don't tell them the name on my driver's license that I use for being normal," Tygeria says.

"Will do," Debbie says.

"So yes, it's a not too large an area, with no other non-missing people around, I can find missing people," Tygeria concludes. "Most people are missing in a crowd, though. If I'm checking a large area with that whole energy vision thing, I can tell living things from inanimate objects, but I can not tell Fred from Wilma. So we're mainly just talking lost in the woods kind stuff there."

"So you can freeze an object, catch it instantly on fire, break down the particles, or 'dust it.' You can scan the surroundings, you can see even when diving fast through the air from that energy vision, and touching the ground to add more energy just gives you greater detail. You can jump from one side of the room to the other if you need. What else?"

"The energy sphere I create to do most of those other things, I also put it in front of me a few feet, and it cuts the wind down. I've been theorizing that I can use it as a shield for bullets, but apparently, that's going to take some practice. It can't do that yet."

"Well, we're not getting much tonight it looks like," Debbie says, "why don't you head home, I'll write the first article. I want us to get something out there soon after that bomb at Central becomes all they talk about all week."

"Now see, that, for example, if I had known there was a bomb in a truck, I could have dusted the whole thing before it went off," Tygeria says. "But they didn't give a bomb threat or nothing, and I guess I'm not sure I would have known where to look, huh."

"That one is definitely not on you. Now get some rest," Debbie says.

Episode 2

P a is sitting in the upstairs media room watching the news. The reporter, Ted Wiley, says," Our top story tonight, Central Command decides to lockdown Earth Central for the next 24 hours following the terror attack earlier today. CCTV shows that it was a white van apparently rigged with explosives next to the retail entrance. The parking garage was not affected, but the main uniform supply store used by their officers is severely damaged. Eight workers in that store are believed to have been killed instantly. There were 20 plus injuries to protesters picketing 40 feet away. No one has claimed responsibility for this attack. Only officers will be admitted to Earth Central campus for the next 24 hours. Civilians are asked to stay away during the cleanup."

As the camera panned across the bombed site, the reporter continued, "This was a parking area outside of security zones, so there is talk that even parking will require security checks before the campus reopens to the public. Most of the retail business is from officers working and training there, so businesses think they will be fine while these changes are made. Services for those killed in this horrific act of terror will be held at the First Baptist Church of Worth on Main Street all day this coming Saturday and Sunday. Supporters have already set up a rough memorial and flowers on the west lawn outside the fence at central."

"So, what is this? A group out there just wants to sabotage the talks between humans and Sanarians?" Tygeria says, walking in behind Pa.

"I guess, a reaction to fear is to make others afraid," Pa says, "makes no sense to me. But apparently, for some, that is logical."

"Watch out for exploding vans while you're out there," Pa jokes. "Seriously, stay away from that sort of thing, you're not indestructible. If you think you've spotted it warn people, call it in, call me I'll call it in. Something but don't get too close."

"Yeah, I don't know what I'd do with a bomb," Tygeria says, flopping down onto the couch.

"Debbie and I were talking it through, and I seem to be stuck with fighting fires and finding people lost in the woods." Tygeria sighs.

"You are way more clever than that, you will get creative with several things," Pa says, "What do you keep telling me, knowledge conquers fear. I think that even applies to your patrols. If we plan ahead a bit and go through multiple ideas about how to handle things and experiment a bit. You can be ready and handle more than you know."

"Well, today, some guys were pulling out an ATM with their truck, so I froze the ATM and their truck, and they ran, but the police were close and got them," Tygeria told him. "But something like that van explosion there was no warning, which I guess is why I just keep circling all evening. Stuff happens so fast, and you only have a brief time to help."

"Well, that's a good point, if you have a way of knowing there is a bomb what would work?" Pa asks.

"Not fire," she laughs, "but I don't know for sure that freezing a bomb would be a safe deterrent, even as instantly as I can freeze the whole van, for example, there are chemicals that might do strange things frozen. I'm curious if just turning the whole bomb and payload to dust on a molecular level would be safest."

"Sounds good," Pa says, getting up, "I've got something for you. I built you an obstacle course in the barn. You've been watching those Parkour videos lets go practice being able to move quickly and jump away since your starting to get into more visible activities. Just always make sure you've got your way out and away when your done helping. Don't go with the police for a statement or let them talk you into getting checked out by the ambulance. Just come straight home if you need help, we'll clean ya up."

"Ok," Tygeria says, and they go take a look at the barn. "What did you do, use parts from the old van?"

"I use everything that was just old and being stored for who knows what reason," Pa grins, feeling quite clever. It's late, so they decide to try it out in the morning.

The reporter, Ted Wiley, comes on TV again, "News from the Earth Central space program. New security measures, work crews 100 officers strong have built a train track connecting the city line one mile away to a platform area to the side of the main security entrance of campus. They have also put in a rail from there to a remote parking lot to the east. The two roads leading into the main gates remain closed and will continue to remain closed. They are planning to reopen to the public tomorrow, and officers and the public are asked to use the remote parking and then take the train into Earth Central from there. There is to be no more on-site parking."

Tygeria understands Pa's point about working with the security team at Central, but for now, she just wants to figure out how everything is working there. She wants an unimpressive job somewhere where she can keep up with the progress they make building the ships and building a relationship with the Sanarians. She settles on getting a position in one of the retail stores that sell souvenirs and educational materials about the space program. She gets the position easily. There are a few more openings than usual since a few people quit their jobs at the stores and shops for fear of more terrorist attacks. It was a small store, so only three employees are working at any one time. Straighten the shelves and run the register, she liked that most of the time she could keep to herself and just say "Hi" to the occasional browser.

She took the train to work every day like most and would always chat small talk with a new person on the train every morning. Her shift ended by three pm each day, so she had time to eat before going to patrol around six pm or eight pm each night until about midnight. This is a pattern she fell into for weeks and then months setting the money aside to get her own place and car by next year.

Within a month, they had cleaned up the damage from the van bomb. They weren't in any hurry to rebuild the store. A new uniform shop was opened in a vacant store space on the opposite side of the courtyard. Every day Tygeria got a thirty-minute break, and she would explore the enormous campus and figure out what happens in each building.

A news report breaks just as Tygeria is heading home from work one day. She watches it on the train TVs. The Reporter, Ted Wiley, comes on TV, "We have breaking news tonight - the joy ride of the century. Someone has stolen a tank from Avian Air force Base, and at this moment, it is traveling 15 mph down I35. Police have caught up to it and are keeping traffic away, but these guys are extremely dangerous. They have driven over and crushed 14 cars on this joy ride, and while we don't have a final count on the fatalities, yes, many of the damaged cars were occupied. If you see this thing coming, get out of the way, I know its tempting to taunt them because they are traveling so slowly, but bullets bounce off and anything trying to block it to stop it will get crushed. Police are scram-bling to clear the freeway completely and hope it runs out of gas before it can hurt anyone else. We have chopper 37 following along on the scene now."

Tygeria gets Debbie on the phone the minute she steps off the train. "Debbie," Tygeria says, "I have to go."

"Calm down, I saw it on the news too, but its broad daylight," Debbie says, "freezing the tank won't work, it won't last. These things run through snow and ice. Coating it with ice will just crack off.

"I know, and I cant dust it either; its way too big to saturate the whole thing with energy," Tygeria says, pacing and thinking. She switches Debbie to the blue tooth headset conversation and walks into a blind corner of the station and takes off straight up into the air too fast to be spotted, then heads for the freeway, and the tank.

"It's a tank, all I have to do is stop the treads, right?" Tygeria says.

"Yeah but it's a tank, there's a lot of weight behind those treads. That's everyone's problem," Debbie says.

"No, that's not what I mean; I mean, what if I dust a few small pins and take the treads off. It stops moving, right?" Tygeria says.

"Yes." Debbie says, "be careful. This is your first full daylight rescue. This will be the first one I publicize, too, hoping to get ahead of the media."

"No pressure though, huh? I'm always careful, talk after," Tygeria says, hanging up.

There are news helicopters following the tank. Tygeria is in uniform, and she glides down and lands on the roof of the tank. She tosses a sphere to the tread and focuses on the pins that connect them. With the snap of her fingers, she turns it to dust on both sides. The tank drives right off its treads and cuts in the concrete and jerks to a stop. The police drive ahead of it guns drawn and get on the megaphone.

"Miss, please step off of the tank. Occupants of tank come out with your hands up." The officers say over the megaphone. Tygeria grabs the lid of the tank, fills it with energy, and then rips it off and tosses it aside. One of the occupants immediately shoots his gun up out the top of the tank. The bullet hits Tygeria in the left shoulder. She flinches and then grabs the gun. She tosses it aside and then grabs the second guy's gun as he stands up in panic inside the tank. Then Tygeria jumps back and off the vehicle onto the median.

"They are unarmed now!" She shouts at the police.

"Wait right there!" One officer yells at her as he points his gun in her direction.

"No thanks, I just wanted to help, the whole thing seemed to be getting kind of crazy," Tygeria answers him.

Aware that they are on TV despite protocol demanding that they secure all aspects of the incident. He lowers his gun and shouts, "Thanks!"

Tygeria takes off straight up into the air. All this prominently and close up was caught on police dashcam and the news choppers. Completely capturing and broadcasting live to the world for the first time ever, shots of her gliding and flying and using her energy on the tank. Suddenly the rumors are a reality, and the world knows there is a superhero in their midst. This worries her a bit because it's a big moment, but she can't worry about that right now, her shoulder hurts and is really throbbing.

The pain in Tygeria's shoulder is so intense she starts seeing double. She climbs high into the air and then slows down and gets her bearings. See points toward home and drops down into a glide, as fast as possible. Thinking the whole trip home about the kind of mess she had gotten into. She's had a few bumps and bruises when she was younger. They seem to heal and vanish within a day. But this. This needs attention. Who can she even go to? She goes to her folk's ranch. Pa can help. They always worry so much that she will get herself hurt. Now look at what she's done. She is dreading those consequences.

Her entire arm is throbbing now. Tygeria lands on the deck on the side of the ranch house. Immediately she drops to her knees. Still in uniform, she calls out to Pa.

Hearing distress in her voice, both parents come running to see what happened. They worry, even more, seeing her still in cloak. Tygeria is always quick to switch out of uniform, so determined to protect her friends and family from being spotted with her public image. This is very out of place. The pain is so intense; she can't focus. She just sits there breathing through the pain.

"Oh, goodness!" Ma shrieks, "is that a bullet? She's been shot, dear. She's never needed a doctor, but now she really needs one badly, and we haven't found someone. If we take her to some random doctor, how do we know they will not make things worse because she's different, or experiment on her, or bad mouth her to the press just to get attention?"

"I've been keeping it in mind; I think I found some-one we will have to start with him and hope for the best," Pa says.

Pa rushes right over beside Tygeria and grabs my her arm. "Here, stand up."

"Ma, grab a towel and some ice and meet us at the car," Pa tells Ma as he and Tygeria start stumbling toward the garage door. Once Tygeria gets into the car, she passes out. Ma sits behind her and holds the ice pack to the shoulder wrapped in the towel. Pa heads to a friend's place. A doctor friend who has a general practice. He will probably be home now, and it's only ten minutes away.

The doctor is an excitable man, always looking for his next challenge. Nothing too hard, or he would have become a surgeon. He just gets his thrills with finding unique cases and telling his friends about how well he handled them. He's quite the talker.

He once told Pa a story about one patient who had trouble hearing, but her own voice and her heartbeat were overpowering and loud in her right ear, dizzy, just weird symptoms. Her old family doctor couldn't figure anything out and just kept blaming allergies, but this guy did a few tests and figured out that she has a hole in her ear, literally. He got in there surgically and plugged the hole with putty or something. Someone who can figure that kind of stuff out can probably do an excellent job of understanding Tygeria.

Dr. Cooper is away from the city in the next town over. He's one of those small-town doctors that has set up an office space to practice in on his property but detached from his home. It works because he is only two blocks away from the main street. It's a Saturday, so he has no business today, and the office is closed up.

"Wait here, let me make sure this is going to work," Pa says.

Tygeria tries to lean back in the car seat a little and closes her eyes, just trying to breathe through the throbbing. Pa parks in the small parking lot in front of the doctor's office but then walks across the yard to the house and rings the bell.

Dr. Cooper opens his front door. He's a tall man with short curly hair. His face looks like a man who has traveled the world. He has light gray stubble for a beard, piercing blue eyes. He's 55 years old, served as a military medic when he was younger. He's wearing a dark gray t-shirt under a sports coat and blue jeans with a pair of work boots currently covered in mud.

"I don't know if you remember me, but we have talked on the phone several times over the past month," Pa says, shaking the doctor's hand. "I need your help with something, but I need to ask you a few questions first."

Dr. Cooper steps out and closes the door behind him.

"Have you been following all the activity going on with the space program?" Pa asks. Dr. Cooper nods. "Have you heard about the person going around in the evenings helping people and stopping fires?"

"Actually, I have." Dr. Cooper stands up a little straighter.

"Do you believe she exists?" Pa asks him.

"I have thought for quite some time that she is our first visitor." Dr. Cooper smiles, "Are you confirming that it's true. There is an alien hanging around helping out?"

"If it were true and she needed your help, would you?" Pa asks sternly, stepping forward right in the guys face a bit.

"All that I can, yes," Dr. Cooper says suddenly, realizing this is not a casual discussion. "She's real, isn't she, she's here, isn't she? I would be honored." Dr. Cooper says. "Let's go to my office, just let me grab the keys."

Dr. Cooper scrambles back into his house for a second, then reemerges fumbling through a set of keys. He looks at the car and spots Tygeria sitting in the passenger seat. Their eyes lock on each other for a few seconds, then he keeps walking to the office door and unlocks it. He quickly turns on the lights and begins to prepare the office for visitors. Pa jogs back over to the car and comes around to the passenger side and helps Tygeria get out. Ma lets go of her shoulder where she was holding the towel tightly, and follows behind.

"Is it safe," Ma whispers to Pa.

"It will be fine," Pa reassures her.

Tygeria, on the other hand, is not comfortable. Not only is she very sore and light-headed, she worries about what this guy will do, how bad will it feel. Not to mention will he then start experimenting on her or something. Logically this will be fine; there's nothing to worry about. Surely with her folks here and everything, she will be safe. This is the first thought, so her nerves are not listening to logic.

They walk into the small office, and Dr. Cooper smiles, and as soon as he saw Tygeria, he spotted the problem, a bullet in the shoulder. He directs them back to his treatment room and gets her settled onto a reclined chair with armrests. Dr. Cooper pulls a stool up beside her and cuts her sleeve away.

"Busy night?" he asks, not sure what to say first.

"I think I should have ducked," Tygeria says shyly.

The room smells like rubbing alcohol with an odd hint of mint in the air. It was comfortable and well lit.

"I was just watching the News when my doorbell rang. I saw you stop the tank. That was pretty impressive," Dr. Cooper says as he pours rubbing alcohol on her shoulder. Then he grabs a syringe of local anesthetic and injects it in her shoulder.

"Sorry, I should have asked first. I'm handling this like you're human, but well, are you?" Dr. Cooper asks, also glancing at Pa.

"My mother was," Tygeria tells him, "so close to just not completely."

"Is there anything I need to know to do differently?" he says, pausing the treatment for a second.

"We don't know much," Tygeria answers, "but I can tell you that shot you just gave me didn't actually do anything."

"It was supposed to make your shoulder numb," Dr. Cooper says.

"Definitely still hurts, just get it over with," Tygeria replies.

Dr. Cooper goes ahead and digs the bullet out and then flushes the wound out with rubbing alcohol again. Tygeria just shakes and keeps trying to breathe through the pain. She learns quickly that she is not much of a screamer. Two stitches later, and he puts a gauze bandage over it.

"Can I take a blood sample?" Dr. Cooper asks.

"No," Pa answers. "I don't see why you would need that."

"Okay, the day after tomorrow, let me check it, even if you need to just send me a photo via text or something."

"Thank you, doctor," Ma says, standing up. Pa shakes his hand again. "Sorry about the strange hour. What can I pay you?

"This one is on me don't worry about it," Dr. Cooper says," I don't know much about, what is it Sanarian medicine, so let's make sure that heals up well. But she should be fine for now. Just take a break for a few days from playing with tanks and things."

"I'm hoping ice will help since the anesthetic didn't do anything." Dr. Cooper says, handing Tygeria an ice pack as he helps her stand up. She takes it, and they head home.

"That went well, right?" Pa asked.

"He seems like he might do ok for us. It's a nice small office, that's good. Can he handle all emergencies?" Ma says.

"If he can't, he would still get her to a hospital anyway which we're facing that possibility eventually anyway, what's the alternative?" Pa points out. "What do you think, do you like him," Pa asks Tygeria.

"I don't think I've decided yet, my shoulder hurts," Tygeria says.

"Does ice help?" Pa asks.

"Actually, yes," Tygeria answers, "but I'm so sleepy."

They get her into bed and let her sleep. The next day her arm is still sore, so she doesn't move it much. Pa checks the bandage, the wound hasn't bled much, but it hasn't healed at all either. Pa decided it would take as much as a week to start seeing healing progress anyway. They take a picture of it every day and share it with Dr. Cooper. By the end of the week, Dr. Cooper suggests giving the whole thing some air since it's not bleeding. So they take all the dressings off and flush it with some water. While he is pouring the water over it, Tygeria blacks out and falls to the ground.

While it seems odd, Pa continues to pour water over it, and the bullet wound disappears as the water flows over, almost as if it were drawn on with paint. There is a subtle hint of the blue glow of bioenergy, so they can tell that it's playing some role in this rapid healing process.

"That's incredible. We just needed to wash it with more water and get all that crap off of there," Pa says." Whatever happened, it made her pass out."

Within 20 minutes, Tygeria wakes up pain-free and stronger than ever. They check her shoulder, and it is black and blue with a dark bruise that ends up lasting a couple of days, but it doesn't feel bad anymore.

"What do you need?" Debbie asks over the phone.

Tyger has her blue tooth headset on for the conversation. "Nothing, I'm fine now, I'm a little groggy, but I figure once I start flying around, I'll feel energized again, figuratively and literally."

"Well, there is nothing on the web or the scanners except word that some rain is on the way so how about you glide around a bit, so you feel better and then come on over and check out the post I wrote, were already getting some responses I think this will work well.

"Okay, I'll bring the food, and we will let it be a day off," Tygeria says, "I've got to get out of this house, thank you." Tygeria hangs up, steps off the back porch, and climbs up to a thousand feet in the cool night air.

There is a slight breeze ahead of the approaching storm. The air is in the 60s, not too cold. Tygeria floats there in one spot just being slightly nudged by the wind, then she spreads her arms out sideways and falls back, letting herself drop for a second. She enjoys the rush, the control, the adrenaline. Gliding is a workout even though she is not running or swimming; it still gets her heart pounding. Her muscles tense up to body surf just right, and her heart is pounding as the levitar flows at full strength, pumping along beside her circulatory system and making her lighter than air. The high-speed drop adds a lot of speed as she pulls her arms to her side and converts it all into a forward motion. She is riding the wind currents like the world's strongest blowing leaf.

Still tired from the previous day's injuries, she has to cut the trip short, so she drops down behind the chicken restaurant two blocks from Debbie's neighborhood and picks up some food for them. Then she walks from there to Debbie's place. Tyger has one of Pa's cars that belongs to her now, but she only uses it to get to work or grab groceries. Most days, she finds herself walking because it leaves her free to fly.

Debbie has a calm temperament with an optimistic view of events. She loves fairs and Renaissance festivals every time they come to town. She paints landscapes when she has free time, bakes and cooks an impressive collection of recipes, and she and Tyger spent their weekends in college hiking the local wilderness trail that was a 12-mile loop. Neither of them hikes anymore, but it's on their "To Do" list.

If Tyger ever had a best friend, Debbie is it. Tygeria would meet Debbie and walk her home any time that week's blind date turned out to be too far from a gentleman. Debbie, in turn, always knew when she would find Tygeria, hiding on the roof of the science building, feeling like too much of an outcast. She would quietly sit down next to her, just smiling, not saying a word. Until Tyger sighed, stood up, and decided to get back to reality. If college is reality. Over the four years they've known each other now, it seems they will always be there for each other.

Debbie has set herself up in the backyard under the covered porch at least until the rain comes later. There is a small fire in the chiminea. She has a couple of Chaise loungers on the porch with a rectangular table between them. She is sitting there with her laptop on her lap, editing what will be the first post about the cities alien visitor. Tyger sees that Debbie is in the backyard as she approaches, so she shouts hello and walks in through the backyard gate.

"I brought chicken," Tygeria says, setting the bag on the table. Debbie scrambles up to her feet, setting the laptop on the table. Oh, thank you. How are you feeling? Let me see that shoulder." Debbie pulls at Tygeria's sleeve and checks for a scar. By now, there is a very dark black bruise radiating out from where the bullet wound was.

"Oh, it's turning colors, that's new," Tygeria says.

"Does it hurt?" Debbie asks, letting go and offering her a seat in the other lounge chair.

"Nope, just a little stiff," Tygeria says.

"That's amazing considering that happened just last week," Debbie says.

"It sure hurt when It happened, but I'm glad it's over now," Tyger says, "so let's see what you've got."

"How about you serve diner, and I'll read it to you," Debbie says, settling back down with her computer.

Debbie reads the post, "As many of you have no doubt noticed by now, our city has a new hero putting in a lot of work. She can do things a little differently, which is why she feels that she must try to help in any way she can. Most of the news reports have ignored or dismissed her, and social media is guessing all over the spectrum. I know her, and we wanted to set the record straight. While many have speculated that she must be one of the aliens from the planet Sarani already here hiding amongst us, you are partially correct. She is not some impostor, her mother was human, and she grew up here in our city, Worth. But yes, her father was one of the many aliens from a place where we are working on expanding relations. And no, he is no longer here. Somehow, this combination has given her abilities that no full Sanarian nor human can accomplish. So she has spent years now randomly helping any time she can. She's shy, so she doesn't do it for the recognition, which is why most don't know about her. However, now that she is helping with needs more publicly visible, we wanted to let everyone know more about who she is. Her name is Tygeria, the blue, silver, and white colors she wears are her family colors. She is not indestructible, but she has an energy force she can use that has helped put out fires. She can use it to lift heavy objects, and like many saw last night, she can use the energy to quickly take something apart like the treads of that stolen tank. Post your questions below, and keep in mind, she just wants to save lives in the few extra ways that she can. And yes, she can fly."

"Yeah, I think that will work. Let's post it," Tygeria says. "I just hate all the talk about all the missing person reports with everyone saying its alien abductions and their proof is the peace talks with the Sanarians. They assume that just because the fleet isn't ready for launch yet that the Sanarians are talking to the officers at Earth Central as a distraction while they abduct people and experiment on them."

"Well, disappearances have gone up. I don't think it's related to the Sanarians though," Debbie says.

"Yeah, I've been keeping an eye out for anything odd like that since we first started talking about it three weeks ago, but I haven't seen anyone being dragged away. And for the record, no flying saucers while I've been up there either." Tygeria says.

"Good job. Keep doing them. The more they can see me as a human, the less afraid they will be in case more stuff happens in daylight that I can't resist," Tygeria says.

Episode 3

"**Y**ou are all over the nightly news from that tank chase yesterday," Pa says to Tygeria as she walks through the front door.

"Yeah, I couldn't avoid the cameras on that one," Tygeria says, "What are they saying?"

"Well, he started by saying apparently the rumors are true," Pa says, "they keep replaying the footage of you flying and breaking the tread on the tank wheels. They reported that the guy in the tank shot at you and you left; then, he mainly talks about the joy ride guys who took the tank. They were all arrested, and the tank is back at Avian Air Force base. There's this guy named Thacher who runs that Air force base. He apologized for the breach of security by civilians, but he also made the statement that if you are a responsible individual, you will register at Earth Central as a cooperative alien. Thacher is blaming Central for their breach of security by letting you through into the world to play."

"Don't do it, of course," Pa says." Just keep on doing as you are. You have every right to be here, just because they don't realize it doesn't let them make demands on you like that."

"Well Debbie posted her first blog so that will clear up the fact that I didn't sneak through Earth Central security to hide on earth, I was born here," Tygeria says.

"How's the shoulder doing?" Pa says, coming over to check. "Wow, that's quite a bruise."

"Doesn't hurt," Tygeria says.

"So I have a question for you," Pa says "since obviously, you're going to keep doing this, do you think you could have picked up the entire tank? How much can you lift?"

"Not sure," Tygeria says." I assumed the tank was too much."

"Come on, let's find out," Pa says. They hop in his truck. It's a 15-year-old Nissan Frontier. They drive to a house that belongs to a friend of Pa and park in the driveway.

"Let's go back here, don't worry, I just talked with him. He's out of town. I told him we were gonna come out here and borrow his auger for some work on our deck. But what I really want you to do is over here.."

This friend had a piece of property just as big as Pa's ranch, but instead of horses, he has cars and tractors and train cars. A lot of transportation items he has collected neatly lined up in hopes of one day opening a museum. They are in a large barn, so they don't get too weathered.

"Start with this one, its small. Just pick it up two feet off the ground and set it back down gently. We don't want to damage any of his collection," Pa points at a VW beetle at the start of the row of cars.

She hops on the roof, uses her right hand to pull open an energy sphere, and then smashes it into the roof of the car. The whole car lights up like it's wrapped in a glowing blue blanket. Then she lifts it off the ground by floating herself up a few feet higher, keeping her hand on the roof. Then she gently sets it back down. They try this over and over again, working down the row to whatever the next significantly heavy vehicle would be. She lifts a truck, tractor, and then when she tries a large school bus at the end that is filled with more collectibles, making it very heavy, she can't even start to lift it. Turns out, it's too big and too dense for her to saturate it with energy. She just doesn't have enough power. Apparently, if she can't saturate all of it, none of it moves. She thanks Pa for the insight, and they go home for the night.

The next evening after work, Tygeria meets Debbie at her place an hour before the sun goes down. They sit at the dining room table, each with a laptop in front of them. Tygeria tells Debbie about the experiment with the cars now that she knows how large an object she can lift. Then together, they search the news reports and social media for any leads on something she can help with tonight.

"Oh, here we go," Debbie leans forward at the table. "A hiker is missing for a day now over in Crocket National Forest. They are stopping the search until morning because it's getting dark. Of course, there is a bit of daylight left, about an hour."

"That's Perfect," Tygeria says. "Ok, so I can find him quickly. I've got better at closing my eyes and scanning just for living things. It doesn't take me long at all to filter out animals and just see the people for a few miles around. I've even practiced counting them. No way to know I'm ever wrong on the count," Tygeria Points out.

"So we've been hiking before, if you need rescue and could only suddenly have things, what things would you suddenly wish for," Tygeria asks Debbie. "After all, I will just have to wait with him until he gets picked up. What should I take."

"Definitely a phone, and he can call the ranger station." Debbie says, "so you need a GPS to figure out his coordinates so he can tell them his exact location. Then I don't know."

Debbie picks up a backpack out of her closet and begins to put items in it. "Water, blanket—let's put a ham sandwich in there just in case, here take even more water."

Tyger puts the backpack on and switches into uniform; the backpack sits neatly under her cloak. Then she heads out into the back yard and takes off into the sky at a rapid speed, which helps prevent her from being noticed during take off while it's still light out. She checks the direction on her phone for a minute and then flies to the forest.

It takes about thirty minutes to get there. On the first pass, all she spots is the team of 20 that are looking for him. Two of them are on ATVs driving on the trails. It seems like they are heading back to the ranger station from whatever part of the woods they were looking for. Then she has a sense of a good spot several miles behind where one of the ATVs is coming from. She turns and glides over to that section, closing her eyes and focusing for a second. She spots him ahead. She opens her eyes and cannot see him through the tree cover, but remembering about how far ahead he was, she glides closer and then carefully drops straight down through a thin spot in the trees. She follows the trail a little further up a hill, and there he is sitting against a tree digging through his pack.

"Are you lost?" Tygeria asks. She is dressed uniquely, but he doesn't see her fly down, so she doesn't strike him as terribly startling, more of a relieved reaction.

"Yes! I fear I've been walking in circles for quite some time. The bridge where I crossed over the is a low water crossing of sorts, and the water rose. I looked for an alternate way back, and now I have no clue how even to find the road." The hiker says.

"Well here, have some water, and you can use my phone to call into the ranger station, I think they are looking for you," Tygeria tells him as she pulls the backpack to one shoulder and swings it around. She hands him the water and the phone. "Are you hurt at all?"

"Mainly just exhausted. My three-hour hike yesterday has turned into a 15-hour endless wander." He says, then he dials the phone and talks to the ranger station.

"Hi, my name is Chris, and I've been lost here in the forest for more than a day now can someone come get me?" the hiker says to the ranger who answers.

"Yes, we have been looking for you, do you know where you are," the ranger asks. "This young lady came up to me and lent me her satellite phone. Mine had no bars and died three hours ago, anyway, so I'm not sure about the location."

Just then, Tygeria holds up the GPS screen showing their current coordinates. "Oh, here it is; we have a GPS too," he reads the ranger the exact location.

They have the ATV nearest them stop and turn back to intercept them. So Tygeria sits down one tree over and offers the guy the sandwich. He gets wrapped up in telling her how crazy his day has been that the time passes quickly. Tygeria can tell that the ATV is getting close, so she packs up the backpack again and tells him his ride is just about here.

"How about you," Chris the hiker asks, "are you just hiking, do you have a camp near here? And should I ask what's with the outfit?"

"No camp, not really hiking, I just heard someone was lost out here, and I like finding lost things."

Just then the ATV drives up the trail behind Chris while he turns to wave at them, Tygeria steps deeper into the trees and finds a clear spot and takes off. From higher up, she waits a bit to see that the ranger on the ATV and Chris drive away after they talk a bit. Then she heads back to Debbie's house.

"Wow, I actually found him quickly enough for them to get him tonight. They are on an ATV and will no doubt be traveling the last bit of the trail in the dark, but they have GPS and headlights and all the stuff they need. He's good now." Tygeria says. Then she takes the pack off and sets it in the corner of the closet. "We should keep that packed; it's the perfect kit. We can just add more water and another snack."

"I will write this one up too," Debbie says. "They have already hit us with so many questions after that first blog post; I don't even know where to begin."

"Really," Tygeria says, her interest peaked. "For the most part, do they sound ok, nobody ready to tar and feather me for being an impostor?"

"No tar, and they are asking if you have feathers," Debbie laughs, "you know the whole flying thing."

"Right," Tygeria says.

"You want to try another missing person?" Debbie asks.

"Did I put the backpack away too soon?" Tygeria asks.

"Probably not, the rest of these aren't hikers; they are just strange, there's a lot of them too," Debbie says. "People that are just gone, their car is still there, purse or wallet often in the car according to police records. The cars were usually found on the side of the roads just parked, not crashed. Some have been gone for months now. I basically just have a list of addresses, but you could walk by the various houses and see if anything stands out to you."

"Sounds good," Tygeria says. "I'll call if I find something."

Tygeria lands in a field a few blocks away from the first address and then walks over to the street she needs. It's a quiet night; a few people are pulling into their driveways. Tygeria just keeps a steady pace walking and looking. There's nothing odd, no one approaching any of the people. She goes to the house of one of the people who disappeared. She can tell the house is empty, so if they have any other family members, they are not here now. She just stands on the sidewalk, looking at the car in the driveway.

When no one is out on the street, she touches the back of the vehicle and focuses on what her energy tells her. This allows her to see not only inside the car but inside its engine, under the chassis, in the trunk, every inch of the car. It all looks perfectly normal. It was towed back to the home, according to the police report Debbie pulled. The keys were still in it, and it was out of gas like it had been left running. The police had done their investigation, and then a family member parked it in the driveway locked up and refueled. Tygeria walks away to a vacant area in the neighborhood at the end of the block and takes off heading for the next address.

She checks ten of the houses on Debbie's list, some with people home, and others not. A few of them, there is no car to check out. All of the police reports are similar. A vehicle left on the side of the road, owner missing never seen again. Purse, wallet keys all still in the car. A handful of them were two people traveling together, and they both vanished. There is no sign of residue, poison, no burning, breakage—nothing.

Tygeria calls Debbie on her headset as she continues to patrol 1,000 feet up in the air. "Yeah, apparently, I'm not any good at this," Tygeria says. "I can't see a thing at any of their homes—nothing unusual on any of the cars. Twenty-three people in the last two months is a lot. I can't believe there are no leads. That's too much to be a serial killer. Are they all from our city."

"Yeah, there's a few more further out west of the city," Debbie explains. "Well, I wonder if we should be looking at possible buildings where someone can house that many hostages."

"Send me some possible addresses, and I'll check the buildings," Tygeria says. "Businesses should be empty at this hour anyway."

On the way back, gliding above the back roads and suburbs on the way home to call it a night, Tygeria spots a car on an empty road pulled over to the shoulder with its lights still on. She glides down closer and realizes that the vehicle is unoccupied, and two people are walking into the field. One is forcing the other.

Tygeria tries to swoop down and catch up to them, but just as she plans to tackle the man from behind, a light window opens up in front of them, and they disappear through it. As she tumbles to the ground, the window of light has disappeared along with the two people she saw. Tygeria takes off and heads to Debbie's instead of home.

"I thought it was strange. I don't even know how to tell you what I just saw," Tygeria says. "We can't publish that either; we are trying to help people not be afraid of aliens, this definitely hurts the cause."

"Why, what did you see?" Debbie says, setting her drink on the counter. Tygeria sinks into one of the dining room chairs. "Um," Tygeria tries to pick her words carefully and then gives up, "I saw an alien abduction!"

"I need a stronger drink," Debbie says, heading to the pantry. She walks Debbie through what she saw with the person and car on the side of the road. "I have no idea how we're gonna figure out the who and why of that," Tygeria says.

"Well," Debbie says, now taking a sip of wine, "What do I always tell you? Let's just handle what we can. Right now, that doesn't seem like one that in our so-called wheelhouse."

"Well, I'm beat. I'm heading home. I have an early work shift tomorrow," Tygeria says.

"Ok, call me tomorrow when you're off, and we will go back to stuff you can handle," Debbie says. "By the way, I managed to get the police scanner band for Austin now too so we can have more to work with."

"Oh good, when I get to go further out like that, I'm getting better at really building up some speed," Tygeria smiles.

"You like the flying part," Debbie says.

"I like the flying part," with that, Tygeria steps into her back yard and shoots up into the air.

Earlier that evening, Dr. Cooper calls Pa on his cell phone. Its the only phone number he has that will reach Tygeria. They talk a bit; he's just checking to see how Tygeria's shoulder is doing and is surprised to find out that water healed it up quickly.

"She had a bruise left behind on that spot for almost a week, but by yesterday even that disappeared," Pa tells him.

"Well, the other reason I'm calling is that I was hoping she could come and let me do a few tests," Dr. Cooper says. "I'd hate to have something else happen to her, and I don't know enough about her body to help her properly, but if I prepare ahead and learn what I can, I will be able to help her better."

"No, I don't want her to become your experiment," Pa answers, "we will just have to handle things as they come. She's Pretty tough and careful. She will be Ok.

I thank you for your help. She will come find you if something else happens if that's Ok."

"Of course, until next time then," Dr. Cooper says. They hang up. Dr cooper taps his pencil on the desk a bit frustrated, staring at the notes on his computer that he has so far. Then he clicks over to another open tab on his computer browser, where he has Debbie's blog pulled up and has made some notes from that about what Tygeria can do and what little is known about how she does it. He has made meticulous notes, and on the pad in front of him are several questions that he now fears will be harder to answer:

How does the Levitra system make her weightless, and can it be synthesized?

Does this bioenergy have unique healing properties, will it also heal a full-blooded human if exposed?

What can weaken her, if necessary?

What do we still have to figure out to help and treat her effectively

The next night, Tygeria knocks on Debbie's door. Debbie opens, saying, "I have bad news, come on in."

"What's that?" Tygeria asks, holding a bag in her left hand and closing the door behind her with her right.

"I can't find a thing out there that's your kinda thing. You could just go patrol and look for traffic issues, but even traffic is light tonight." Debbie says.

"I have a different idea," Tygeria says; she pulls a box out of the bag she brought and sets the box on the table.

"Chess?" Debbie says. "Revenge match, huh? You actually think you can beat me this time."

"Definitely. I think I just choose the wrong color last time. This time I'm playing white." Tygeria says.

They set up and settle in for a long game that takes all evening. The whole time they discuss Debbie's new guy who does supply deliveries where she works. Debbie is old fashioned enough that she really wants the guy to ask for the first date. It's frustrating because he's taking too long. So far, Debbie has learned that he likes cars, he has a Doberman, and he goes fishing on his days off. She tells Tygeria that she saw him again today. He only comes once a week, and she dropped a hint that she's been dying to see the new movie about the guys who designed the Shelby GT. He did not take the bait. Then Debbie wins the chess match.

"Well, I'd better head home," Tygeria says. "Speaking of, guess what. I found a good apartment three blocks from here, so I'm about to get my own place. I saved up enough. I can still swing by the Ranch every other weekend and make sure Pa doesn't need help moving something big. He's pretty much got everything converted into retirement mode, so there won't be much more of that."

"Nice," Debbie says. "Well, you helped me move into this place, so just keep me posted, and I'll come help you pack or unpack. Or watch… you know whatever."

"Yeah," Tygeria smiles then leaves.

Over the next few weeks, Tygeria switches between patrolling and packing. Its mostly quiet, nothing big enough for Debbie to add to the blog.

Two weeks later, Tygeria has mostly moved into her apartment. She still fusses about what things are going to go where, but she's fresh out of college, so aside from a hand me down couch and a new set of dishes Ma gave her, she doesn't have much so there's not much to fuss over.

Tygeria is riding the train home from work, and everyone starts watching the sky to the east. There is a lot of smoke off in the distance. Tygeria gets off at the next stop, walks behind a nearby building, and takes off above the smoke. It turns out it was from many miles away. On the far side of the forest, there was so much smoke visible because the area on fire was huge. It was the far side of a large forest area, a wildfire, and very high winds were making it much worse. Tygeria gets Debbie on the phone as she glides down for a closer look.

"I can't put this out; it's too big," Tygeria says. "The forest is on fire and its spread through a small town, I can't tell which town from up here."

"Ok, let me pull it up."

Debbie is at her home and hasn't seen the smoke from where she is, but she opens the back door and can smell it. "Wow it's got to be huge, I can smell it in my backyard."

"Not helping. I know its huge, that's the problem," Tygeria says. She is circling the smoke cloud, trying to stay out of it.

"Ok, first of all, don't think about putting the entire fire out," Debbie says, "you're here for people remember. They are trying to evacuate using Main Street and Vine Street. Go see if that traffic is moving or if they are fire blocked. There are mixed reports about Vine Street maybe being blocked.

"Well, I can't see street signs from here, but I can tell where all the people are concentrating on the roads. They are just bunching up; if they get trapped, they will burn," Tygeria says.

Tygeria starts gliding low and slow. The wind is strong, but if she lets it blow her west, that is where the new fires are popping up. Entire trees are entirely engulfed in flame. A bright orange glow is the only break in the thick smoke that makes the day look like night. There is a crackling sound all around, not a crackling, a roar, some combination of the flame, and the wind roars like the forest itself gasping for air.

The McDonald's is on fire, but the building beside it is not. Across the street the gas station is burning. Roads cannot act as a fire break when the winds are this strong. Entire burning branches are being blown off the trees and landing a block away, jumping the fire forward.

Tygeria follows the line of cars. Everyone is huddled in their cars with the windows rolled tight, trying to keep the smoke out. They are all trying to stay calm, waiting for traffic to move. The heat is unbearable. Tygeria has lived in Texas all her life, so 100 degrees on a windy day feels like walking in an oven. But this is so hot it hurts to breathe. Tygeria heads to the front of the line of cars, trying to evacuate and sees the problem. Burning trees have fallen across the road waiting for the fire truck to try to get there. She lands on the far side of the fallen trees.

She takes the white scarf off that she usually wears on her head and wraps it around her head to cover her mouth and nose instead. Her adrenaline is high, so she has a lot of built-up energy. She knows she will need every bit of it. She finds a stick on the ground that is cold, and she fills it with energy and then touches it to the closest fallen tree. The energy flows from her through the stick and into the burning tree across the road. She can tell when the tree is saturated. With a snap of her fingers, the tree turns to dust—nothing left to burn. It has broken down at a molecular level and fallen apart. With no fuel left, the flames disappear.

She hits tree after tree using the stick to get closer until the road is clear. There is a police car on the other side, parked blocking traffic from the hazard. The officers are slack-jawed watching her. One finally speaks, "Wow, thanks, any chance you can extinguish this whole mess?"

"No faster than that," she says, "one tree at a time, and I'll run out of juice after 20 trees, so trying to figure it out."

"Oh, ok," the officer says.

"Are there any other roads blocked?" Tygeria asks.

"Yes, Main Street is blocked right before the freeway access. A burning building has blown and spread across the road," he says, pointing north.

Tygeria jumps up about 30 feet high and falls into a low glide again, flying along barely higher than the cars.

She gets to the freeway and sees Main Street. Sure enough, a hardware store is raging in flames. All the cars in the parking lot are burning. The sample sheds that were displayed along the edge of the lot have burned down to the base already. The main building doesn't have much roof left. Smoke coming from the building has an assortment of different smells because of the burning of household chemicals that filled the shelves. There is a variety of materials in the road burning but nothing that can be easily touched. Tygeria uses her headset to call Debbie again.

"Did you say there was water near here?" Tygeria says.

"Yes, a lake north of you about five miles away. In fact, you're at the northernmost edge of the flames," Debbie says.

"Perfect, maybe I can put my energy sphere in the lake and expand it to some manageable size and freeze all the water inside it and carry it back here. I don't know how big I can manage, a ball the size of a car, I suppose."

Tygeria heads to the lake and follows her plan. The ball of ice follows her in tow back to the hardware store. Then she applies her heat to the large sphere of ice, turning it back to water, and the whole thing makes a glorious splash onto the burning road in front of the store. It works. It puts out everything that was burning on the pavement. She signals to the stunned people standing in the street to drive past while you can, and she goes back to the lake to grab more water.

This time, she drops the water on the store itself. It makes the smoke worse, and then the flame consumes it. She tries again, heading back to the lake to get more water. They have water helicopters working there too, and she sees one in the distance heading to refill its bucket. She heads to the hardware store and drops this batch of water on the parking lot instead of hoping that it will keep the road open.

The smoke blowing across the road increases, and the cars stop for a few minutes until its clear again. The parking lot is not just a sea of twisted metal, but she can tell there were no people in them. The area had been evacuated on foot somehow. That's when she notices that some of the cars on Main Street are empty but blocking the others now that the road fire is out. A few officers and two civilians are starting to push one of these off toward the shoulder of the road.

Tygeria jumps on the roof of another one, picks it up and floats it over into the grass, and drops it. Then she gets the abandoned truck and moves it too. The guys pushing the sedan have stopped and are watching her. She lands on the roof of the vehicle.

"Want me to move this one off the road?" Tygeria says to one of the officers.

"Please, yes. Thank you," he replies, "stand back, guys, let her move it."

She Pulls open a sphere, smashes it into the roof of the sedan, and then flies up a few feet and lets the wind blow her and the car sideways into the grass where she drops it. Then she takes off again to see what other groups of people she can find.

Homes everywhere are burning. Behind the fire, smoke slowly rises as if rising out of the earth itself. She passes what is left of a school and a church. She's behind the fire line in the destruction area and checks for any signs of people. There are cars in driveways with burnt skeletons in them. How hot must this have been to do that?

She tries to focus on all the safe people. She goes back where she can sense life and panic happening. She works for five hours straight long into the night, turning trees to dust, moving cars, dropping water where it might help. It feels like putting out a camp-fire with a squirt gun. Eventually, the town is evacuated, and the fire line is heading toward the center from several directions so that it will burn itself out at this point. She is exhausted and ready to head home, but on the way gliding around the edge of the smoke, she spots the shape of a small child huddled in the corner of a barn.

The barn itself is already burning in a smoldering way, not a raging flame. Tygeria lands near the barn door and runs in through the few flames that lick the door frame heading right to where the boy is in the back. He has cleared all the hay out of one of the stalls in the back, so there is nothing but dirt, hoping this will help protect him. Tygeria runs back to where he is, "Hey, can I get you out of here? Where are your parents?"

"They aren't home yet; we can't go out there. It's all burning. There's too much smoke." He says, running over to her.

He's not the least bit scared. "You can help me. I've seen you on TV."

Quickly, Tygeria pulls her phone out of her pocket and takes a screenshot of the coordinates of their location.

"How would you like to fly?" She asks him.

The barn is popping and creaking, and the flames by the doorway get brighter. He comes over to her, so she picks him up on her hip and carries him out of the barn. Just then, a falling tree crashes through the roof of the barn right across their path. Tygeria jumps out of the way of it and the material falling with it, holding tight to her little passenger. She instinctively blocks with her left arm, and it gets scraped and burned a bit by some of the beams from the roof. One of the larger pieces hits her right leg, feeling the bruise, she jumps backward deeper into the barn.

"You ok?" Tygeria asks her passenger.

"Yeah," he says.

"What's your name, little man?" she asks.

"Bobby."

"Hold on to my neck Bobby," she says.

He hugs her neck, and she uses her right hand to freeze the main part of the tree that fell in front of them. Then she climbs past it underneath and out the front door of the barn. Then she takes off holding tight to Bobby. Debbie directs her to the nearest hospital outside the disaster area, and she drops him off there. She lands by their emergency door, pulls a piece of paper and pen from her pocket, and checks the coordinates that she saved earlier, and writes it on the paper.

"He was in the back of a barn at this location," she wrote.

Then she told bobby to take the note and go inside and find an adult. A nurse was already heading through the doors toward them, so Tygeria walks away and continues to head home. Her leg is throbbing, and she limps when she lands at home. She goes quickly into the tub and starts to rinse off clothes and all. As she peels away the layers, she can see that she's bleeding more than what the water can handle, so decides she should see if Dr. Cooper can help with this one. She changes into clean, dry clothes and heads out.

It's about 9:30 at night. She lands in the empty parking lot in front of Dr. Cooper's office and walks over to his house. She rings the doorbell but then walks several feet back away from the door. Dr. Cooper opens the door.

"Yes," he answers, "oh, hi, It's you."

He closes the door behind him, reaches in his pocket to check for his keys, and then starts walking toward the office. Glancing back behind him, "Can you walk ok, your limping?"

"Well enough, but yeah, it hurts." Tygeria answers.

"What kind of disaster did you find tonight? "Dr. Cooper asks.

"Forrest fire, burning through a town. A barn roof collapsed on me," she says.

"Ok," Dr. Cooper says, holding the door of the office open for her. "Come on back."

He checks for cuts that haven't closed and turned to bruises and flushes them with water. Then he waits a while to see if they stop bleeding on their own without bandaging them. Most do. He checks her leg. He tells her it doesn't seem broken, but there's a lot of swelling, it took a good hit. He can tell she's sore and agitated, so he offers to inject a sedative, but she declines. So he says he needs a blood sample and without waiting sticks a syringe into her arm and draws blood.

Once he pulls the needle out, she sits up, "Hey, give me that! I said no!" Tygeria says.

Without missing a beat, he continues, "Just one more." he says, this time instead of drawing blood, he gives her a sedative after all, and she falls asleep.

When she wakes up, she is alone in the exam room. She checks her watch. It's three am. An ice pack is wrapped around the swelling on her leg. She gets up and looks around the room, and finds three blood samples labeled alien hybrid stored in the cold case in the hall. She goes into the door marked as his office and right on his desk are the notes questioning her weaknesses, etc., and a list of tests he's going to do on the blood samples.

The doctor is in the house, not sleeping despite the late hour, searching for something, probably expecting her to be still asleep. Then someone pulls up out front in a pickup truck. The doctor goes to meet him. She's frustrated that he seems to be crossing the line into experimenting on her instead of helping her.

She decides as she flips through an alarming amount of notes from every possible research source, asking questions and making speculations about how her body might work. She grabs the book once she realizes it has no records about other patients. Notes about her are in a separate book from his usual note-taking. She grabs the blood samples and leaves out the back door. She knows she will not use him ever again and needs to find a new doctor.

Dr. Cooper approaches the man in the truck, "are you general Thacher?"

"Yes sir, is she still here?" Thacher asks.

"Yes, I have her sedated, she is inside," Dr. Cooper says.

"Thacher turns the truck engine off and steps out." You're doing your country an excellent service, these people are dangerous. They are responsible for most of the disappearance plaguing our city. They are acting like heroes, so we won't suspect what they are really up to. We just need to take her back to the base and get some answers. If we are about to join the theater of the people of the universe, we are going as a dominant species, not some slave race."

Tygeria gets home too sleepy to fill in Pa or Debbie, so she just packs some more ice on her leg and gets some sleep.

Episode 4

A tall man with a military look, army navy store, not actual service, walks into a concrete building at a rock quarry. He has short curly black hair, high cheekbones, and a chiseled chin covered by a well-groomed beard.

"Can I help you?" says the man behind the counter.

"Why are you the only guys offering top money for this stuff?" the military dressed man says.

"What can I say; we have a unique buyer," the flannel shirt behind the counter replies." Are you looking for a job?"

"Not quite," the stranger says.

Just then, another gentleman steps out from the back. He's wearing jeans and a button-up shirt. "You asking about limestone? What kind of heavy equipment can you operate?"

"None, what is the heavy equipment for," the stranger asks.

"Well, the amount of limestone we want isn't the kind of thing you can just you grab a shovel for," he says.

"I own some property near here that we, what do you call it, excavated? Lots of limestone for the land before we built our home. Will you buy it? I can use a little cash." The stranger explains.

"Even better, is it all broken up, were going for rocks one-foot diameter or smaller," he says, "We're just loading up the rock hauler trailers, we'll hook them up to the trucks when they get back from the last delivery. What's your name, stranger?"

"Tzorion (Tz-rye-N)," the stranger answers.

"Well, that's an odd name, I'll just call ya Ryan if that's OK, my name is Adrian. Come out here. I will show you where you can bring it."

They step outside. Adrian shows Tzorion a row of empty rock hauler trailers, no truck attached. "I pay by the truckload. Fill one of those, and you won't have to worry about your bills for a month. So you got a big piece of land around here?"

"Yea, it's a little ways away but not bad," Tzorion answers. "So who's this buyer of yours that needs all this anyway?"

"You into all this interstellar development we've got going on these days?" Adrian asks.

"I follow it a bit," Tzorion answers.

"It turns out that limestone can be used to make that rocket fuel that makes all of Central's plans get up and go," Adrian explains.

"That's surprising that you can sell it at all. I'm not quite sure why Central didn't just buy up all the limestone quarries in the country if it can make rocket fuel," Tzorion ponders.

"That's because they don't know, they are still using their first blend of power cells to run the fleet they have almost finished building up there in orbit. This is black market stuff mostly, the other guys are using, and if they knew this planet had so much limestone, one of the key ingredients in the process, this planet would be having a lot of close encounters," Adrian says.

"The other guys, huh," Tzorion asks.

"Well, you know. That's what my buyer thinks; as long as he's paying good money, I don't care how crazy he is," Adrian says.

"Well, I'll bring what I can by morning then," Tzorion responds.

"Sounds good. So you must be from around here then?" Adrian asks.

"I was an orphan, bounced around from foster home to foster home when I was young, I'm not from anywhere," Tzorion replies. "In the morning, then."

On the Army base, Thacher is walking down one of the hallways when his phone rings. "Hello," he says.

"I'm ready," the voice on the other end says. Its a low-level officer calling from his garage at home. He is in uniform and zipping up a heavy object in a Central duffel bag.

"You're clear to proceed, call me when it's done," Thacher says.

"Yes sir," the officer says.

Then he starts his car and drives to the train parking at Central, catching a train the rest of the way. He doesn't head through the usual entrance but instead heads around with a few other officers to a side door that leads directly into the machine shop area where the pre-build on the engines is being done. He heads over to a workstation near one of the massive engine components for the ships that are being built.

He checks to make sure no one is looking, and he ducks around the back of the engine where no one can see him. Working quickly, he removes an explosive from the duffel bag and sets it inside a void space of the engine out of view. He starts a countdown timer for thirty minutes, and then grabs the empty duffel and hurries out of the building and back on the train.

He is sitting in his car, watching as a counter on his phone counts down to zero. Nothing happens. He waits an extra 30 minutes then calls Thacher.

"Hello," Thacher answers.

"Nothing? I set it for 30 and waited 60. Nothing," the officer says.

"Are you saying it didn't go off?" Thacher whispers angrily into the phone.

"It didn't go off. There must have been something wrong." The officer says.

"Fine, OK. Fine. Double-check the other one," Thacher tells him."We have to wait a few weeks before we try again."

"Understood." The officer says. He hangs up.

Tzorion is sitting in his cabin, looking through news articles about the forest fire. The report is filled with pictures and stories of the people who lost friends and loved ones. It is also filled with articles and photographs of Tygeria helping and stories of people's gratitude.

"Well, if she can run around without having to hide," Tzorion says to himself.

He switches over to the live news feeds. There is a report of a semi that is out of control nearby. It has hit a few cars and is still barreling down the road at top speed. He changes into a black uniform and heads that way. Tzorion has a different gliding style than Tygeria. It is ridged, unpracticed, stiff. He finds the semi that is being chased by police cars at this point. He lands on the roof.

Tzorion has enough power to saturate the whole semi with energy, even at top speed.

"Well, I know what will stop you from crashing into anyone," Tzorion says to himself, and then he dusts the whole thing.

Dusting can never affect a human being. So the driver of the truck suddenly finds himself with no seat under him nor truck around him. As he starts to fall to the pavement below, Tzorion reaches through the dust and grabs the guy by his belt and flies him straight up out of view, then takes him back to his compound unseen.

The whole thing is captured on police dashcam, and the news reports explode with stories about a second alien who is destructive and taking people. Speculation starts that he is the one behind many of the cars on the side of the road disappearances.

"These aliens are getting out of control, and here we are trying to set up some big conference with them," Thacher yells at a table full of agreeing listeners.

They are not at the army base, and no one is in uniform. They are in an office building downtown. The anti unification symbol is on a flag hanging on the wall behind him at the head of the table.

"We need to figure out some way to be the ones abducting them instead," Thacher says. "I can't control what those yahoos at Central are doing, and hopefully one day they will come to their senses. After all, they have deadly jobs. But I say any alien already daring to operate outside that barrier is undeniable trespassing and is fair game to be hunted down and caged."

The people around the table cheer and agree, pounding the table and yelling.

"We can't let them mix with humans. They are too powerful, and power corrupts, as you can see. We need to continue the work we are doing to slow them down at Central. We need to get press coverage on the protests and point this exact stuff out as a reason to shut that place down. This city, actually, this country needs to take risks more seriously, and nobody is talking about it."

A large group of protesters gathers outside Central again, and news teams interview them.

"These aliens can destroy anything they want with a snap of their fingers; we can't allow that," one woman says to the news interviewer. "Central says they have everything secure and under control, and yet new aliens keep popping up every day doing whatever they want outside the barrier," another gentleman says.

The reporter corrects him, saying that two different people are hardly a new one every day. The crowd erupts with fear and yelling; the protests continue for the rest of the week. Some of the members of Thacher's terrorist group are walking amongst them, talking fear into people's ears. They don't have to protest themselves; they just have to keep making others afraid.

Thacher meets with the officer who placed the bomb. They are at the downtown office space standing beside the meeting table. No one else is there right now. Everyone else is with the protesters.

"You have a working one this time?" Thacher asks him.

"Yes, we should be all set. I can't get it to the right place until they finish the rest of the install. They are set to launch the ships next week. They are just putting them in orbit. I figure this time if I use the ship's circuit board itself as my trigger, we won't have to worry about any faulty switch," the engineering officer assures him.

"Good," Thacher says," The Sanarians are coming in a month for the big meeting, we don't have a lot of time left to persuade these guys to call the whole thing off."

"I understand, this will work," the engineering officer says.

The week passes, and Tygeria continues with her usual evening patrol through the city. When Worth is too quiet, she goes further out to the next town. She spots a collapsed cell tower that has crushed two work trucks. She can tell people are still inside. Police cars are approaching, but no cranes or equipment to help has arrived.

Tygeria lands on the top of the cell tower wreckage near the trucks and energizes a few feet of the tower, then flies up and tosses it aside. The base is too heavy and never moves, but this gets the tower off the trucks, and the whole twisted mess now lays off to the side on the ground. The police have parked nearby and are running toward the guys in the trucks.

Tygeria lands and speeds over to the first truck. The guys inside pull back from her a little. She can tell the cops that were coming up behind her stop, she turns to look back at them, and they take a few steps back. She sighs and puts her hand on the driver's side door and converts it to dust.

"Can you get out, OK?" Tygeria asks the men.

They don't answer; they just look at her, clearly afraid. She does the same with the door on the other truck. The police have their hands on their guns and still have not come any closer. She steps back from the second truck and then shoots straight up into the air. Once she is too high up to be seen, she looks back down and watches to make sure they get everyone out of the trucks. As soon as she leaves, they spring to action, and everyone gets out with minor injuries. An ambulance is already heading up the road, so she leaves and heads towards Debbie's house.

"They are afraid of me now," Tygeria says to Debbie as they stand on the back porch."They literally back away from me, and nobody would talk."

"Really!" Debbie says."You had made so much progress."

"I can't believe there is someone else out there like me, after all," Tygeria says.

"Well, we knew that was entirely possible. You spent most of your time in college searching the web for others, convinced there were more hybrids." Debbie says.

"Looks like I drew one out," Tygeria says."Except the jerk is giving aliens a bad reputation now."

"I know," Debbie says."People react with fear first, but that seldom lasts. You just keep doing good work, and we will keep spreading positive news, and people will come to their senses that people are different, and they make their own choices. They should be afraid of him apparently. But they shouldn't be frightened of you. They will see that, give it time."

"I hope so," Tygeria says.

"If you want to go right back to interacting with people less," Debbie says, "Then do that. Just don't stop helping."

"OK," Tygeria says."Well, nothing is going on tonight."

"Oh good," Debbie gets up and grabs the TV remote off the coffee table. "Come on in, change clothes. Its officially movie night. Should we watch war of the worlds? Kidding. Just kidding how about that documentary they aired last week about touring the new starships that are about to launch. Those things are floating cities, have you seen it yet?"

"No," Tygeria says, "I was working when they showed that one."

"Let's watch that; I'll get the snacks," Debbie says.

Tygeria switches from her uniform to jeans and t-shirt and sits down in the recliner clearly still agitated. As the documentary plays, she and Debbie start talking about all the wonderful things that might be out there and how neat it would be to live on one of the ships for a year.

Episode 5

That evening, Tzorion comes back to the quarry where he talked to Adrian, and he walks down to the bottom of the pit and puts his hand on the wall. Bioenergy flows through him into the wall. The energy traces its way through the limestone, drawing lines that would break the limestone up into small enough boulders. Then Tzorion steps back away from the wall that is still glowing with energy, and then he snaps his fingers. The lines turn to dust, and the material that surrounded it has been carved into the small bits. The limestone tumbles down onto the ground in front of him. He walks to the large landslide of a pile and places his hand on it again. Once again, it glows with bioenergy, and then he floats up into the air taking the pile in tow behind him and dumps it into the first empty rock hauler. Within an hour, he fills up ten of them. Perfect size perfect cut, right from the guys own quarry.

The next morning Tzorion comes back for payment. Adrian is stunned. How did he fill these so fast? How did he get it all here? A deal is a deal, so Tzorion was paid well for his supply. "Let me know if you need more," Tzorion says.

"Seriously," Adrian says. "You've got them perfectly shaped and everything, it takes us two days to break, cut, shape, and fill just one trailer. If you've got more that looks like that already, you can load up for me; I'll take all you've got."

"Well, first, you need more empty trailers," Tzorion points out.

"True, tell you what, gave me a week to deliver those to my buyer, and then I can call you when I can take more," Adrian advised.

Tzorion pulls a card out of his pocket and slides it across the counter, "My number."

Tzorion sits in a recliner in front of a fireplace. He checks his bank balance on his computer to confirm the payment. Its a small log cabin on a large piece of land many states over from where the quarry was. After all, just like Tygeria, Tzorion can fly. The cabin runs off solar power and well water. It is dimly lit with dark heavy curtains covering the windows. The shelves are filled with books and hunting weapons hanging from the walls.

The floors are hardwood and give the place a constant, subtle smell of pine. The pine is masked by the smell of rotting flesh from the two corpses sitting in the corner, half turned to dust. You see, Tzorion didn't go to college and get a job; instead, he worked construction jobs and slept in a hammock in abandoned buildings. Then he took this place from a nice young couple that was boondocking and wouldn't be missed.

On one end of the property, he has a massive construction project underway. It's going to be as large as a school, some rooms are done, and others have only a foundation. He is slowly building it himself. But thanks to bioenergy helping him with heavy lifting, he can tackle the project all on his own. He uses the money from the limestone sale to buy the rest of the materials he needs and still has money left over.

He switches screens on his computer to a physician chat. The latest experiment results were negative. Please come in for more tests or at least send another blood sample. That's the end of the message. Tzorion's hands start to shake, but he puts the computer aside and heads back out to the construction site to resume his work. Three hours pass as he works on the frame to pour the next round of concrete.

Tzorion's hands start to shake as he tries to hold his tools. He sighs and decides its time to take a break.

Halfway back to the house, he passes out on the trail into the woods and is left lying there.

A small space cruiser with powerful engines is traveling at hyper speed just beyond the planet Sarani. The Captain is the only one on board. It's a small ship that can carry a little cargo—that's why he deals in precious minerals that fetch a high price per pound. Captain G squirms in his chair. One hand holds a steering wheel, and the other is reaching down to a pack on the floor beside his chair. He pulls out a metal thermos and pops off the top with his thumb, then one-handed he brings the thermos to his lips and chugs four large gulps of the fermented liquid, letting some of the resulting froth drip into his full beard. Captain G lets out a satisfied ah, its a good ale. He balances the large flask on his knee, watching his main screen, carefully skirting the edge of the range that the Sanarian sensors from Central can detect. He doesn't want them even to see him, he's just passing through and needs them merely as a landmark of sorts.

The ship has a small cockpit and four staterooms for the crew. Captain G has his things spread out between two of them. The rest of the vessel is all cargo space. It's modest in size, so he usually makes sure he deals in high dollar low volume cargo, which lately is limestone shipments. The planets that reached space travel status four decades back and started plan-

et-hopping were all run off a fuel that has a dirty man-
ufacturing process and several chemical and natural
ingredients. It has become popular because it does not
use any of the same resources that the various planets
tend to use to run their infrastructure. After all, we are
dealing with different physics in space.

Limestone tends to be the most significant necessary ingredient, and because of that, it has also become
scarce on most planets. Deposits that are left are the
hard ones to get too, the bottom of the oceans, etc. So
the freelance suppliers have started going further and
further out trying to find new sources of untapped deposits. There are rumors that there is an entire moon
made of the stuff somewhere. Its become like searching for the city of Atlantis. Only half-believed, but it
keeps driving hope of easy riches. Sarani has a few
untapped limestone deposits, but they have it well se-
cured against smugglers, and the gravitational and at-
mospheric differences on the planet make it very hard
for outsiders to do much for long term visits.

Captain G heads out further than he has been before, his sensors spot a vast space complex orbiting a
blue planet, so he heads that way to check the resources of the surface. He circles the planet to the far side
away from the space complex and its potential security, and then he pierces the atmosphere on the dark
side and picks a field for landing. That's the beauty

of these cruiser ships; they are made for planet-hop-ping, so they are the right size for setting down on the surface among the trees somewhere and exploring around.

This field that captain G picked happens to be half a mile away from where Tzorion is building. Tzorion watches in awe as the ship touches down. Most would not be able to see it in the dark, but Tzorion has bio-energy and energy vision, so he sees precisely what it is and wonders what kind of opportunity it might be. He shoots up into the air and then comes just high enough to angle so that he comes straight back down next to the ship. It's dark, so he is hard to spot but also worth noting at this point that he doesn't bother to hide.

"If you are here to abduct me, I have bad news, I've already cornered the market on snatching up hu-mans," Tzorion says.

"Sorry, mister, I don't mean no harm. I'm just a test pilot with your space program, and I had a little trouble." Captain G says.

"No you're not," Tzorion says.

He walks right up to captain G and stands nose to nose with the guy. Captain G takes a step back and clears his throat. "Did you say you're abducting peo-ple?" Captain G says.

"Let's handle your truth before we get into mine. This is my property, after all," Capitan G says. The Captain holds up the computer in his hand and flips through the screen. "Half human half Sanarian, well, isn't that interesting?"

"Let's just say my mother was out of this world," Tzorion says as he starts to admire the captain's ship.

"Does that mean you need a ride?" Captain G asks, "Are you trying to go find her?"

"She's dead. The military of this world shot her," Tzorion explains. "All I want to know is what you're doing on my property?"

"I can move; my apologies. It was a temporary stop; I just need to handle my cargo a minute," Capitan G says.

Tzorion lays his hand on Captain G's ship and closes his eyes, "You have no cargo?"

"That is because I'm still handling it. That limestone over there, is that your land too?" Capitan G asks.

"Why, do you need some?" Tzorion asks.

"I'll buy it from you; it's an important ingredient in hopper fuel," Captain G says. "Now those big flying cities this world is building up there in orbit, those take a different kind of fuel as I'm sure they have figured out. But a little ship like mine here can run on hopper fuel, and the hardest ingredient in the manu-

facture is limestone. Low and behold the newest planet in the arena that is space trade and travel had a crap
ton of it they seem to hardly never use."

"I think we can talk some business," Tzorion says.

Capitan G invites Tzorion aboard his ship. "So,
what do you do with the humans you say you're abducting?"

"I've got this condition," Tzorion explains, "and so
far, the only thing I found that fixes it uses cells from
a human liver. And then, you process it using Hydes
#1 serum. I have plenty of the serum, but I need a new
fresh liver every time I make more. Every two weeks, I
have to grab someone. An old doctor friend of mine, a
pure Sanarian, helped me figure out the formula. I decided that the livers of the recently deceased were not
pure enough; in fact, compared to a healthy live liver,
the formula made from the cells from a live liver last
seven times longer than what we were getting raiding
morgues."

"But Sanarians don't have livers. They have two
organs that do similar work, but it's not the same
thing as a human liver." Captain G says.

"Exactly, which is why I had to stow away back to
earth and live here on this underdeveloped dump, so
I've always got a fresh supply," Tzorion says. "So Humans can't survive with their liver removed, so body
disposal is also difficult."

"Does this ship of yours have some sort remote access to get on board, or is landing your only option?" Tzorion asks.

"There is a transport window on it, yes," Captain G replies.

Tzorion smiles, and then goes on board and takes a seat. Tzorion fills Captain G in on plans to build a compound where he can stash several people at once and save them for later while learning everything he can about the strengths and weaknesses of this new species {humans}.

Tzorion also tells him how easily he mined the limestone. Captain G proposes that he use his ship to get Tzorion a large instant spread out selection of humans to put in his cages. And Tzorion gives loads up the entire cargo hold of his starship. It would be an even trade. Then Capitan G will come back for more limestone and get Tzorion more people. The journey to sell the limestone on the black market to the right destination will be a two-month round trip. The two men agree, and Tzorion offers to give Captain G his first load free while Tzorion finishes building his cages, and in two months, he will be ready.

"Just keep in mind your one load behind always, you owe me until we make other arrangements, and if you don't hold up your end, I have contacts in this larger arena that will hunt you down," Tzorion says.

"You also need to take the bodies with you on the cargo ship, dump them in space for all I care I just don't want anyone giving me trouble here."

"No worries," Captain G laughs. "It's a good arrangement, and I would talk to you before we go our separate ways. We would settle up first, but for now, I like the idea of getting rich. I take it these Humans don't put up much of a fight, huh?"

"Feed them the right lie, and they won't even go looking for the truth," Tzorion laughs, "the few people that know me think I'm here to rescue them."

Tzorion loads up Captain G's cargo hold, and the Capitan takes off into the night sky out into space on his long journey to his buyers. Tzorion returns to his work on his compound, now determined to finish it within the next two months before the Capitan gets back.

Debbie is in her living room. A laptop is set up on the coffee table, and she watches a blue dot travel across the map. Its the GPS signal from Tygeria's phone. Debbie is still looking out for any events, but it's a quiet night, so she just keeps a lookout on Tygeria's location. She switches on the TV to see if the news has anything interesting.

The reporter, Ted Wiley, is on mid broadcast, "Well, I guess people won't be eating there anytime soon. In other news tonight, another missing person case this time over on Hawthorne Dr. near the Arts District. Mr. Goldberg's car was found on the side of the road. It looked like he intentionally pulled over, there is no sign of struggle, and there is no damage to the car. Police are continuing their investigation, but they did say that Mr. Goldberg's keys were still in the car, he did turn the engine off before he got out. They have not found any other tire tracks even though the area where Goldberg pulled over is very muddy. So muddy in fact that there is one set of footprints presumed to belong to Mr. Goldberg that leads from the driver's door around the front of the car and down the ally nearby. Then they just stop. We will keep you posted if there are any further developments. This does match an ever-growing list of missing person cases this year. We are constantly noticing a pattern of five every month."

Debbie makes a few notes about the incident in case it can help them, and then she flips through the channels to see what else is on.

Back at Tzorion's compound, he is working on the structure and comes to a stopping point for the night, so he puts his tools away. Then he walks to the far end of the compound where some of the rooms are complete and pulls a set of keys out of his pocket and unlocks the door in front of him. He walks into an area designed as a kitchen where he has a pot of water over a wood fire that has just recently come to a boil. He grabs a ladle and scoops some of the water into a bowl. Then he grabs a container of oatmeal off the counter and pours some into the hot water. He gives it a little stir but leaves the spoon behind on the counter, then extinguishes the fire. Then he walks across the hallway and fiddles with his keys once again. He unlocks that door, and walks into the room, turns on the light.

It is a large room, made of a combination of metal and concrete. There are a few chairs and buckets in there. In the corner sits Mr. Goldberg, cowering and afraid to approach Tzorion. Tzorion tosses the bowl of oatmeal down in the middle of the large room and walks back out. As he leaves, he speaks to Mr. Goldberg, "don't worry. It won't be long. I will finish dealing with you tomorrow."

The door closes and deadbolts lock again, but this time the lights are left on. Mr. Goldberg scrambles over to the bowl, and realizing its just oatmeal, he uses his hand to eat every last bit. He has not washed in two days and has bruises on his face and arms. There is a bucket of clean water in the room with a ladle in it, and Mr. Goldberg takes a drink. Then he lines up three of the chairs and uses them as a bed platform, no covers, no pillow. He falls asleep.

Episode 6

Tygeria went to her folks' house to help them with some chores on the property. She was mowing the lawn at the ranch on a mild spring morning. There are a few clouds, and the weather report says it's going to rain most of the rest of the week, so she is trying to get the grass cut before the storm gets there.

She parks the mower in the shed beside the barn, and steps into the barn. Tygeria is still limping, her leg swollen and tender, but she's moving around on it a bit, hoping that in a day or two, it will be good as new. Pa is standing over at a workbench repairing one of his favorite saddles.

"I can't use Dr. Cooper anymore," Tygeria says, "he's not safe."

Pa drops his tools and turns with a serious face, "What happened? What did he do?"

"He drugged me even though I said not to," Tygeria explains, "then he drew several blood samples apparently even though he had already asked if he could, and I already said no. I got the blood samples and his notes about wanting to figure out what effects this and that and what can hurt me. I took everything he had relating to me and left while he was out front talking to that head commander at the army base. The same guy who lost his tank to a bunch of joyriders."

"Feeling OK now?" Pa asks, checking her arms and hands, "I'm so sorry, I thought he would be safe. Do you think he was gonna harm you, or was he just messing with samples?"

"Just messing with samples." Tygeria answers, "I do think he was gonna pass me off to that Thacher guy from the army base."

"My biggest fear is someone starts torturing you just to see what makes you tick," Pa says.

"It's so frustrating. I just want some aspects of my life to be normal. I want to be able to turn it off and do things the way everyone else gets to. Go to a hospital if I bash my dang leg, I want to be able to join Central Security instead of hiding out as a cashier in a gift shop. I love helping with some of these disasters," Tygeria says.

"Let me ask you something," Pa says, "who do you want Tygeria to be. Are you going for superhero status? Fame? Acceptance? Pride?"

"Pride a little probably," Tygeria says, "no, I don't want to turn into some celebrity, which is why I try to do so much while staying hidden. Then Debbie can blog the credit to helpful aliens, and people will get excited about these contacts Earth Central is starting to make. I want to be an ambassador for Earth when all that gets underway. I want to make sure other aliens that do inevitably come along don't mess things up by trying fear and oppression. I guess I just feel like I'm the only one who can stop some of them, so then I feel guilty if I don't help with disasters and bad people."

"I love that you help and that you want to help," Pa says. "But you don't need to feel obligated to help. If someone is running around misbehaving, abducting people, that's on him; you are not obligated to fix it. That said, it is a good thing for you to help, but don't feel guilty if you can't."

"But I do feel guilty," Tygeria says, "I know I can do things, so then I feel guilty if people get hurt because I what, decided not to go."

"OK, you do you, I will keep helping you train and problem solve. Do you want me to try to find a new doctor you can use?"

"No," Tygeria says, "I think I'll try to find one on my own somehow."

"OK," Pa hugs her, "you can always come by here day or night, and we will do our best to help patch you up."

"I'll be careful too," Tygeria says.

"So the other day, you said you saw someone taken through a window of light," Pa says. "Do you think its one of the aliens doing it?"

"I've never met another alien," Tygeria points out. "But that was really strange."

"Learn what you can," but don't you go disappearing in the process. None of those missing people have ever been found or returned."

Tygeria's phone rings, "There is a lot of tornado damage about 3 hours away, you interested?" Debbie asks.

"Yeah, send me the coordinates," Tygeria says.

Tygeria is at the ranch, so she shoots straight up into the air really high and then glides down steep. Then she slows her fall turning all that speed into a smooth forward motion. She can keep climbing a bit and falling again to keep the momentum going. This lets her cover the distance in about 30 minutes. She flies right into the storm and rain that she was preparing for. The small drops of rain soak her cloak, but it keeps it from stinging her skin as she flies.

The first thing she spots is some large trees that have been uprooted and tossed across the freeway blocking traffic. She lands on the far side that is away from the cars hiding behind the debris. She walks up to the first tree and opens up a sphere and tosses it into the tree. She places her hand on the tree, and the entire thing glows as it becomes saturated with bioenergy. With a snap of her fingers, the whole thing turns to dust and blows away. She moves to the next one and repeats the process. A few of the people have stepped out of their cars and are trying to watch through the debris. For the last one, she still prefers to keep her distance, so she walks to the far end of the tree in the median and dusts it from there. A few people in their cars start to hoop and holler, and one yells, thank you in her direction. She takes off again to see what the heart of the disaster looks like.

Further in she finds a pocket of streets where the roofs have been ripped off of houses. She lands at the end of the road and bends down, putting her hand against the ground and closing her eyes, she checks all the homes for people. She can tell that they are all out front and in the streets, and no one is left inside any of these, so she takes off again and follows the debris trail.

She checks an isolated house that has toppled onto itself like fallen dominoes. There is the strong smell of natural gas and oils in the air from the damaged lines and cars etc. The wind is still blowing mildly, and the rain has not stopped.

She touches the ground and scans the area spotting someone under the debris. She heads right over to where the person is and starts moving waste and tossing it aside. She comes to a large beam in her way and turns it to dust like she did the trees. She can hear the person shouting for help now that he hears movement. A few more pieces of rubble and she sticks her hand into a crawl space, and the young woman crawls out from under what used to be her bed and into the open air.

"Oh my god, my house!"

"You OK? Anything broke?" Tygeria asks her.

"No, I'm fine."

The young lady is so stunned that she doesn't even react to Tygeria's appearance in her cloak. She just stands there stunned, looking at all her stuff scattered to the wind. Tygeria says, "Step carefully. I'm gonna go check your neighbors."

Tygeria flies off into the dark sky as the rain starts to pick up. It's a cold rain that stings as she glides through it. She sees at the local school that the roof of the gym is gone, so she lands and checks it. There are 12 people in there, and they were all cold and dead, most of them crushed by concrete. She scans again,

hoping shes wrong. This makes her look more close-
ly at each of them as her energy passes through the
building. They are all gone, and those who survived
have gone elsewhere. The rest of the building is empty, and the rest is remarkably untouched.

"This is quite a mess," Tygeria tells Debbie.

"It looks like your down to rain, no sign of any
more tornadoes forming as the storm continues,"
Debbie says. "Did you find anyone yet?"

"I cleared the trees off the freeway and got one person out of a toppled house. Even though it's dark and
raining, there are a lot of people walking around outside, assessing the damage," Tygeria tells her. "Hang
on. There are some cars tossed off the road over here.
I'm gonna check them."

"OK, be careful, don't get hit by lightning or anything," Debbie says.

"Don't say that; you'll make me worry about lightning. I worry about that sometimes," Tygeria answers.

Tygeria spots a retail street where the bank and
the church have had their roofs ripped off, and a few
walls have fallen. Tygeria lands and scans that street,
spotting two dogs and a person in the auto shop on
the corner that has no damage, there is a small grocery
store with 15 people in it watching the weather from
just inside the door. There is no damage to that building either. The police station on the end, has a base-

ment level to it with the computers and communications from there. She can tell most people are still at their computers and on phones talking to people trying to help coordinate officers to get to those who are injured and need rides to the hospital. Three of them are near the stairs and door trying to get it opened, but it's blocked by a partially collapsed wall above.

Tygeria rushes over to the police station to help. There are bricks and filing cabinets in a pile leading to the door they need to come and go from the room where they handle 911 calls. She starts throwing bricks aside as far as she can toss them and then uses her energy to move the larger bulky items. It takes almost an hour to move enough to get to the door. Tygeria pounds on the door and shouts, it's almost clear, hang on. The guys inside shout back that there are 21 people in there.

The officers on the phones manage to coordinate the officers out in the field working. While none of them were planning on leaving dispatch until their work was done, they needed to be safe, and they needed to be able to come and go. Tygeria was eager to check and make sure the other walls seemed sound, but she didn't want to stop moving rubble yet. Gradually she cleared enough room for the door to open and a pathway leading through the debris out to the street.

Once the door is free, she opens it and says hi and asks is everyone OK.

The officers are stunned but relieved, so they just say, "Yeah, no injuries, is the building solid?"

"Of course, yeah, we're good," the officer nearest her says. "Hey, by the way, what's your name?"

"Tygeria," she answers, and then walks back toward the street and takes off again.

Her arms are tired from all the constant lifting debris. She knew there was more ahead, and she wanted to keep checking.

Tygeria has landed while they talked and is checking the cars. There are three of them. Only one person is lying beside a vehicle that is sitting on its roof. She could see in her mind's eye that he didn't register as a person. She's usually already aware of people around her because of the energy coming off them. Living things and objects look different. Objects are dark and cold, with no heat or life coming off them. This gentleman looked like an object as Tygeria approached. To her eyes, he just looks like he layed down to take a nap. She checked him, and it turns out he was dead. That explained the strange appearance.

"That guy didn't make it, but there is no one else there," Tygeria tells Debbie.

"You found someone dead? " Debbie asks.

"Yeah," Tygeria says.

"That's rough. I'm sorry, send me the coordinates, and I'll report it so you can go find your next one." Debbie says.

"Yeah, OK," Tygeria answers. Debbie can tell she's getting rattled a bit by the scope of the mess. So she tries to help Tygeria refocus, "Did it hit any larger buildings?"

"Good point, let me check," Tygeria answers as she shoots back up high above it all and looks at the overall path that the tornado had taken.

A black jeep is sitting on the other side of a field. Thacher sits inside, holding binoculars watching Tygeria check people. Since those where she stopped were already dead, he wonders what she's doing. He's been chasing around from disaster to disaster, assuming he can start following her that way and recording what she is doing. When Tygeria flies away again, he starts his engine and heads in the same direction.

Mainly the storm passed through the edge of two neighborhoods, a few farms, and fields and clipped the corner of one car dealership near the freeway. About ten empty cars were picked up and tossed about half a mile away. The rain lets up, and Tygeria cannot find anyone else stuck inside any of the damaged homes.

"I don't think I have anywhere else I can go now. There are police cars on all the affected streets talking to the people." Tygeria says to Debbie, "they are all starting to get into clean up mode now."

"Well, good job, come on back," Debbie says.

"How's the weather?" Tygeria asks, "If I head back north, am I just going to fly back into the storm, those winds are more than I can glide through?"

"Yeah, yeah, hang on, let me give you an alternate route," Debbie says. She checks the weather on her laptop. "Head east until you cross a freeway again, and then you can come north. That should take you around it, and it's heading away from you to the west anyway."

"Great, thanks," Tygeria answers and takes off following Debbie's path.

When she spots the freeway below and turns, she sees the big black storm off in the distance behind her. It's impressive and terrifying at the same moment. She takes a second just hovering in mid-air, thousands of feet up just watching the heart of the storm dump lots of rain and flooding on the small towns and fields in its path.

She sighs and continues home. She says goodbye to Debbie and turns her headset off. Tygeria lands on the outside patio and grabs a throw off her favorite chair, wrapping up in it, trying to dry off and warm up. She throws a fire sphere into the fireplace and lights the logs.

Pa walks out and comes over to her, "you look like you've been running around in the rain."

"Yeah, I'm just trying to warm up and dry off," Tygeria says as she sits down on her favorite chair.

She is thoroughly exhausted. She doesn't want to lift her arms anymore; they are so sore. She is still shivering, trying to let the fire warm her.

"Was it rough?" Pa asks.

"It was sad," Tygeria says, "it was a just a mess, couldn't prevent that, just trying to get a few people out. Several were already dead. That's so creepy. I just kept wanting to find people alive. And I did, a few anyway and it felt so good. I know I started this just because I wanted people to 'generally' like aliens as their first instinct instead of the pop culture notion of aliens are here to conquer. But that mission aside, I like just helping people anyway. Initially, I was just hoping somehow I could live a normal life. Not hide so much, I'm not sure normal is what I want either. This is not normal, but I like it."

"You are doing good work, we will keep working on your defenses, and this can be your normal as long as you don't settle in so much that you let your guard down. I'll make you some hot tea," Pa says, heading back inside.

Pa brings the hot tea and hands it to her. She sips it, and gradually the shivering stops. "Come on in; you've had a long day."

An engineer carrying an Earth Central duffel bag walks down the long hallway and boards a departing shuttle. It drops off its passengers at the main dock of the space station. Officers and engineers are walking in all directions busily finishing up details. The engineer with the duffel steps off the shuttle and crosses the lobby area to the elevators. The space station has artificial gravity, so within its walls, people can move normally. The elevator takes him up to a long hallway with several access tunnels. These are all lined up with the starship access doors and air locked to the ship. He enters the ship by the propulsion room. They designed the vessel to have separate propulsion power versus the engine room that just powers the ship itself to keep this floating city running.

He is the only one in the propulsion room. He sets the duffel bag down by a massive computer panel on the wall. Besides this panel, there is a sticker on the wall that says "caution volatile fuel behind this wall, no flames allowed." He pulls a screwdriver from the duffel, exposing a tattoo on his wrist that is in the shape of a crossed-out union symbol.

The union symbol shows when Sanarians and humans when they first met. It looks like a cylinder with a large ring floating off of each end. It is not their symbol but instead is shared among the five known species in the universe to show that they are cooperatively sharing the space between worlds. Earth Central has already worked the union symbol into some of the flags and uniforms being sent out into this shared space.

The engineer unscrews the clear face cover of the panel. Then he reaches into the duffel and pulls out a cylinder with two wires coming out of one end. He pulls one end of tow wires free in the panel and twists them to the cylinder wires. Then he tucks the cylinder down at the base of the panel. He closes it all up, grabs the bag and tools, and leaves the way he came.

Downtown Worth has very tall buildings. Tygeria loves gliding through them because the wind can get fast. It's been two weeks since the tornado. Her leg is fine, and the city is bursting with activity in the spring weather. Two of the four-star ships are scheduled to leave the dock and settle into an orbit around the planet. They will fire up their engines for the first time at noon today. Once these two are moved out of the way, the other two can park in the station for their last check. The occasion will be broadcast live on television, and they will also show shots of the command deck as the crews take control of their ships for the first time.

The news is calling it a pre-launch, and its the first public look at the first finished ships. There are watch parties planned everywhere. Restaurants advertising eat your lunch here and watch the pre-launch. All eyes will be looking at the first step for the future of humanity. As Tygeria glides above the city, she closes her eyes to practice quick counting people only to realize thousands surround her. She has the day off work but decides to glide over Earth Central to see what they have planned for the pre-launch.

There are large crowds in the central courtyard watching the TVs that are mounted on posts throughout. The lines to buy food are the longest she has seen. Banners are decorating the halls celebrating the completion of the first two ships. The other two are slated to be finished by the end of the week; then all four will be put into service on Saturday. These celebrations are bound to last all week as a result.

The launch unfolds on the televisions with everyone watching. The bridge crews take their positions. The power supply for the ships has been running during construction. Now they just need to turn on the engines. They talk their way through the power-up, and the first one starts moving forward out of the space dock. It waits until its clear of the dock, then it moves faster and enters a high orbit around earth. Then the second one does the same. The ships are massive, but they look small and manageable on the television screens. They hold a crew of 4000 when they leave on their year-long mission to explore and see the other populated worlds galaxies away. For now, they only carry a bridge crew.

As the second ship switches to faster speed, we see the panel in the propulsion room. The one that the engineer wired to the cylinder. The lights light up, and once the process triggers that circuit, the canister explodes. It was highly explosive, and in turn, triggered the ship's fuel cell, which was just behind the caution flammable sign. The entire ship blows apart within a series of five chain reaction explosions. The large, lightly populated upper section of the ship is thrown further out into space, but broken up pieces of the engines get tossed into the atmosphere and start to fall to earth like meteors. These fuel flaming pieces are enormous. Tygeria sees them in the upper atmosphere from where she is and races up toward them. She can get behind some of the larger pieces and manages to turn them to dust. A few, she can tell, will land in the ocean, and she ignores a few that are headed toward a field. She chases the rest, destroying as many as she can on the way down. Trying to get to all of them before they hit, but there are too many pieces.

It was a relatively small piece that hit the buildings downtown, but it brought a heavily fueled fire with it. The hole in the skyscraper was five floors high. The building itself was an office complex that was 50 stories high and took up the space of an entire downtown block. The impact hole is about halfway up the east side of the building. Chunks of concrete, metal, and paper rained down from the building as an increasing amount of smoke bellowed up. People on the dining patios at some of the restaurants stand and look up stunned. As rubble falls near them, they jump up in the seats and start running inside for cover. People on the streets stop walking to watch. Those that work on the lower floors feel the building shudder and start evacuating to the first floor and out into the streets. Traffic is brought to a standstill for four to five blocks around the building.

Something hit the building next door also. It is only five floors high, but smoke starts billowing out of the windows there also. The distant sounds of fire alarms sounding in the buildings fill the nearby streets. Joined by the sirens of approaching fire trucks and police all coming to help evacuate the premises. On the streets, there is confusion about what hit the buildings. People are holding up their phones, taking video and pictures as the disaster unfolds.

Tygeria decides even though she failed to catch and destroy enough of the falling debris, she needs to stop the fires in these two buildings that the debris caused. She glides around the building looking at the damage. Flames and smoke are billowing out from the impact hole. On the opposite side of the building, the windows have all been blown out, but the smoke is going the other way. She darts in through one of those broken windows and lands inside the building. All the furniture and most of the walls are all dust and ash already, the heat right there is unbearable. Her cloak gives her some protection, but she realizes quickly that she can't stay here long, so she jumps back out and enters the building on a higher floor. It is still hot but not as bad.

At least three floors are engulfed in flames. Air rushes in through the gaping hole in the side of the building, causing fire to be pulled up elevator shafts onto the upper floors.

Tygeria can sense that all the people still alive are packing the stairways and the roof, or they are down on the first three floors waiting and trying to leave among the crowd. There is thankfully no one on these floors. She fears if she doesn't put the fire out, people will be trapped on the roof too long until the fire catches them. So she ramps up her power and pounds it into the floor she is standing on trying to freeze the whole floor. It quickly melts and heats right back up within minutes. She checks the second building, and people are still scattered throughout, struggling in the low visibility to get off the floors through the smoke. She decides to head over to that building and try to put that fire out first; this one is too large for her to make a dent.

The smaller building has walls and furniture more intact, but it has all been pushed over to the far wall in a mess of a pile from the impact shock wave. People are crawling on their hands and knees toward the doorways. She lands on the third floor and uses her energy to break a bunch of the windows to let more of the smoke out. People can see better, and she tells them to keep going, get downstairs, and leave. Then this time, she froze the floor above her, and some of the fire is out as a result. Steam mixes with the smoke, and the air starts to clear even more. Several people are trapped behind some desks that have pinned a door closed. She heads over and dusts the three desks one at a time, then pulls the door open and tells them to get low and get out. They thank her and scramble past. The firefighters are working their way up the stairwells as the people come down. Another crew enters the taller building to make the long climb up. They know they can't put the fire out either, and at this point, they just plan on containing it on those floors until it burns up the fuel and puts itself out.

Then the ground rumbles and shutters as if a large train just rattled past down the hallways. Ceiling tiles drop down, and the office workers start screaming and running faster into the stairwells. Some people get trampled. Then the unthinkable happens. The 50-floor office building starts to fall sideways. The center has been weakened too severely. The building drops sideways quickly and crushes the smaller office building. Parts of the concrete are turned to dust. Dust and smoke fill the air for many blocks, coating buildings, and people.

Some get out of their cars and leave them, and everyone starts running from the toxic cloud. When the dust settles, there is nothing left of either building but a four-story pile of twisted concrete and metal, and the fires are out. No sign of Tygeria, no sign of the firefighters who went in, nor any of the people who were still lined up to get out. Many of the people who had just evacuated and waiting in the street, were now cut, bruised, and covered in ash.

The city catches its collective breath and slowly walks back toward the mess, trying to decide where to start to get people out and clean up the mess. The sirens have all stopped. There is an eerie silence that the city has never known—a cloud of ash hovers. The world looks as if it turned gray. For blocks, shop windows have been blown out from the shock wave from the building collapse. Merchandise, tables, deli counters, and shopping carts inside these stores are covered in ash and concrete dust. People start handing out water bottles to those covered in ash who are slowly walking away from the disaster. The first responders are wetting cloths and tying them around their mouth and nose and walking back toward the rubble.

Tygeria latched her energy onto some pieces of the wall around her when it all started to fall. She was able to shield herself and is now trapped under tons of metal and concrete. The pocket of space is just big enough to move her upper body a bit, but her legs are pinned under some twisted metal. The metal protected her legs from the impact but now holds her trapped. She can't reach it to dust it and free herself, so she starts dusting a few other pieces around her. Quickly this starts making the whole pile around her shift and threatens to crush her, so she stops.

She scans the building from where she is closing her eyes and focusing. How many people do they have to get out? She can find the few people on the edge of the pile, about five of them total. No one else. Where did they all go? How did they get out? She is confused. Maybe she blacked out and didn't realize it. She can tell police and firefighters are starting to dig through the pile. So she decides she just has to wait for them to move more debris so she can safely free herself.

Her side hurts, bruised ribs probably. She is frustrated with herself; she didn't help any of these people. She just became a victim right along with them. She prays this event won't ruin the space program. What made that ship blow up like that? She tries to get her hand to her pocket, and she grabs her phone. It won't even turn on, and the screen is cracked. She keeps it close in case Debbie can still track her with it, but she can't call out. It's quiet and still. There is a toxic chemical smell, and then the smoky smell. There isn't even a breeze.

Several hours later, the news is still covering the disaster, and the announcement goes out that a bomb went off in the ship, triggered by the propulsion system firing up through its various stages. Once it was labeled an act of terror, the worry about trouble with the other ships subsided. The propulsion systems on the other ships were inspected for tampering. None is found. They still make plans to orbit the vessels around the moon instead of using Earth's orbit just to be extra safe.

The teams keep cleaning up and searching for survivors all day long. As night approaches, they bring in large floodlights and shine them onto the mountain of rubble that is two city blocks large. Word starts spreading that they are not even finding bodies, just body parts, and the country falls into a state of collective mourning with the realization that hundreds died in an instant, including the city's primary firefighting teams.

First responders from all over the state responded and started taking shifts helping dig and remove debris. Their spirits are lifted when every once in a while, a victim is found alive on the edges of the debris pile, which is still one story high. Now and then, everyone working stops and they all get quiet. One fireman will yell out, "Is anybody there!" and everyone listens for yelling or tapping or any movement.

Each time there is nothing but silence. Tygeria is too deep in the middle of the pile to be heard or to even hear them. Trapped and tired, she falls asleep. Gradually the workers, one by one, go back to moving and picking up debris. They repeat this every thirty minutes, hoping to find people alive.

Ma and Pa watch the coverage on TV. Everyone knows that Tygeria went in to help. Thanks to Debbie's blog, most of the population has come to recognize her and the work she is doing. So most are holding their breath as the news keeps repeating that she is lost in the rubble and feared to be dead. Eighty-eight people, 14 firefighters, and one superhero presumed dead, crushed by the buildings that collapsed in downtown Worth.

Pa keeps reassuring Ma, "She's still alive, don't worry; she's still alive."

They decide they need to go to watch and wait. So they pack up the car with bedding, food, and supplies to they can camp out in it on the street and help with the disaster.

Busses arrive on the scene and pull as close to the middle of downtown as they can. Then forty Earth Central officers get off, each carrying gloves and buckets. They walk the rest of the way to the debris area, quiet and in three main lines almost like a march but not. The whole incident is too somber. The first responders that are already there are starting to tire already and are grateful to see reinforcements coming. The officers are all in uniform and wearing masks over their mouth and nose to keep from breathing in all the dust. Carefully they step onto the pile of rubble and spread out, picking up pieces and filling their buckets, looking for survivors. They are determined that at least Tygeria can survive this, and they feel obligated to help her as though she is one on their own just because she is gradually being accepted as the Earth's first alien.

Ma and Pa stop at a store on the way downtown and buy ten cases of bottled water, as much as they think the back of the truck will hold with the bed cap on and all their other gear. They even packed a fold-

ing table and a couple of chairs. When they get downtown, they go over by the hospital that is a few blocks
away. There the nurses and doctors scrambled to prepare as much space and equipment as possible for a
flood of victims that never came. They're some of the
first responders come over from the work area for a
break. The nurses are trading out masks for them and
offering chips and sandwiches. Ma and Pa set up the
table they brought and filled it with bottled water for
anyone who wants some. They take the water grate-
fully.

The citizens are slowly leaving the dusty area after checking on their businesses. The people working
on the debris pile take several bottles so they can take
some back to the site to give to others still working.
The workers come and go in waves, and in between,
Ma and Pa set up their chairs and sit waiting. They
have tried Tygeria's phone several times. It just keeps
going straight to voice mail. Pa just keeps trying.

Water drips down on Tygeria, and she wakes up
again. Now, most of the smoke around her has cleared,
and sunlight peeks trough above her, way above her.
She can't believe how tall the pile of twisted metal is.
She whistles loudly, but the workers above her just
keep working. No sign that they could hear.

She tries moving again. One foot wiggles free, so
she finds a small piece of rebar near the other leg and

dusts it. This gives her just enough room to move both legs and start sliding out from the puzzle where she is trapped. She crawls into an open space, coughing from all the dust she is stirring up. Then she carefully starts climbing to the sunlight over and under big blocks of concrete, large and small twisted beams. She carefully watches where she puts her hands and feet because it's too cramped to float, and she doesn't want to slip back down. Near the top, she has a large open area to pass through finally. So she opens a sphere and throws it up to saturate the top layer of debris where she assumes she will punch through, and then she flies up and through the top of the pile.

She shoots out of the top of the pile, debris scattering as she breaks through. She goes only high enough to clear the top of the pile by a few feet. Then she glides down, skirting the top edge, mere inches from some of the rescuers until she reaches the street beyond where all the equipment and support are set up on the surrounding sidewalks. She tumbles to the ground right in the middle of the dusty road and lays there exhausted, looking up at the beautiful sun. She thinks to herself she didn't help this disaster one bit, but at least she got herself out. The bright sun is almost blinding. Rescuers and Earth Central officers rush over to her with wet rags and oxygen, blankets, and a backboard.

She is too tired to run, too tired to worry, too tired to be afraid, too tired to even talk to them.

"It's OK, you're out," one of the rescuers says. "Just lay still we will help you," he reassures her.

She closes her eyes and leaves herself at their mercy, knowing, for the most part, they want to help, but do they know how? They take her to the hospital a few blocks away, and the reporters gather at the doors.

Ma and Pa are relieved for a moment, but new worries creep up. They just want to get to her, but the medical staff isn't letting any of the reporters or bystanders in, and they know they can't just claim to be her parents, no one would believe them anyway. They decide if they stay there, they will at least get all the updates.

Tygeria opens her eyes. She finds she is on a hospital bed in a small room. A window allows the sunlight in, but the door is closed. A table and chair sit in the corner. A man is sitting at the table with a clipboard in front of him. He sees that she is awake, and he calmly stands up and moves to a chair beside the bed, bringing the clipboard with him.

Tygeria enjoys the comfort of the soft plush bed compared to being stuck in the pile of broken concrete. She worries what is on this doctor's clipboard, what test will he insist on doing?

"Hi," he says as he sits down beside her. "I'm Dr. Blue, but you can call me Mark if you would like. Do you remember what happened?"

She nods. Tygeria sits up a bit, and Mark just sits there, not writing anything, not making a move. She checks her arms, no IV's or needles.

"We have you on oxygen, " Mark points out, "and there are a few ice packs tucked here and there that seem to be helping with the bruises. I'm impressed. You had a building dropped on you, one that crushed everyone else so much that no one has been found whole."

Tygeria cringes as he says this, "Sorry," he says. "But impressively enough, you didn't break a single bone."

Tygeria keeps glancing at the clipboard, trying to see what kind of notes he has. He sees this and turns it to her and shows her whats on it. I've just been tracking your blood pressure. I'm trying to see signs of internal bleeding, but at this point, I think you're OK. You're a little low, see," he points to the pattern of numbers. "But it has been going back up not down."

Then Mark sets the clipboard down and leans back in his chair, "You don't trust doctors, do you?"

"Not so far," she says.

"I'm sorry," he says. This confuses and surprises her. "That means they haven't been helpful. I'll admit even some of my colleagues here have taken a hands-off approach. They are not afraid of you; they are just scared of not knowing enough."

"You're not afraid of not knowing enough?" Tygeria asks him. She squirms and settles in a little more comfortably.

"I figure you need someone. I just can't walk away from the opportunity just because I might be in over my head." Mark says.

"You're not in over your head," Tygeria reassures him, "I don't hurt easily. But I suppose I keep running into the big stuff, so I keep getting banged up anyway. Usually, it all heals with a good cleaning and a little time."

"Good," Mark says. "Speaking of…What hurts?"

"I'm fine," Tygeria says.

"Tough, huh," Mark smiles. "How are your lungs, can you breathe OK?"

"Yeah, sore throat, I guess," Tygeria says. "My side hurts a bit, but only when I breathe really deep."

"That would be the bruised ribs." Mark says, "I wanted to let you wake up before I gave you anything, do you want to try a pain killer?"

"Experience says my body will just neutralize it, no effect," Tygeria says. "Really, it's not too bad. I'm stiff more than sore."

"OK," Mark says. "Do you have someone, family maybe that you want to call?"

"Yeah, in fact, I can tell they are outside," Tygeria says.

"I can bring them up," Mark offers.

"No, " Tygeria says. "This is too public for that. I would just call them, but..." she holds up the smashed cell phone.

"Here, you can borrow mine," Mark hands her his phone.

"Sorry, thank you, but that would leave too many traces. I think I trust you, but there are too many others out there who would give us no peace if my family and home were suddenly public knowledge." Tygeria hands it back.

"I get it," Mark says. "What can I do?"

"Just go tell the crowd down there, in case anyone is worried that I'm fine and resting," Tygeria says.

"They are in the crowd, and your family will hear that," Mark says, understanding as he stands up from the chair. "But will they believe me?"

"Probably not," Tygeria laughs.

He heads downstairs and announces to the crowd and the media that Tygeria is recovering well, nothing was broken, she just needs time to heal. Then before he comes back up, he walks into the hospital gift shop and makes a quick purchase. Then he heads back up to the fourth floor and goes into her room.

"Here, let's see if we can move your sim card over." Mark says, cutting open a new prepaid cell phone, "you can keep this."

That got her. Tygeria decided, with that, he can be trusted. She pulls her phone back out, and they get the replacement phone working.

"I'll give you a moment. I'm going to set up at the nurses' station. You press that button, and I will come back in, granted if one of the lady nurses needs to help you with something, let me know. If you get too sore, I have more ice at least, or we can try something else if you have ideas. Otherwise, just get some more sleep, and I'll just make sure no one bothers you," Mark says.

"Wow, thank you," Tygeria says wholeheartedly.

"Good people are out there, Tygeria," he says. "You should know that your one of them." Then he closes the door behind him.

She calls Pa and tells him she's safe. She will come home later tonight after her lungs stop burning. They plan on rushing back home, so they will be there when she slips out. But not now, for now, she closes her eyes and sleeps.

She catches the news report and realizes for the first time that all those people were crushed out of existence. Eighty-eight office workers, 14 firefighters,

killed in one afternoon. Five survivors plus one superhero.

Episode 7

"I'm sorry," Pa says. "It is my job to protect you, to raise you, and protect you. And you're so unique, so I thought that meant I had to work harder at it. So I taught you to hide. But your heart wouldn't let you live a quiet life, not interacting with others. So I fear I may have unknowingly taught you that others' opinions of you matter."

"To some degree, you're right," Tygeria says.

"NO!" he interrupts. "You're living a reactive life, and it's all my fault. You're worrying about what Tzorion is doing and reacting to him. You're fixing his mess because you think you have to. You're fixing his image because you think it matters. You're reacting to the terrorist attacks because you think it's on you to do so because you're the only one who can do something. Don't live reactively. And when you're not working hard at all that you're hiding, you're hiding from people, hiding from doctors, hiding from ever just fully being yourself. Even under that cloak, you're hiding as you help people. Stop hiding. Stop being reactive. You go be you."

Pa walks over and takes the plate from her hand and sets it on the counter. "Tomorrow is your day off of work, right?" Pa asks.

"Yeah," she says. She's breathless, almost confused by the conversation. He is solving a problem she didn't even know existed, and that's a new one for her. She can't always do better, but she usually knows what needs work.

"Tomorrow," Pa says, gently sitting her down at the table, "just, go downtown or something, put your cloak on you do still need a pinch of anonymity so you can get groceries. So keep the uniform, stand on top of some building, close your eyes, and find the world around you. Then you do whatever it is your heart needs to do. Not because it's good for the image, not because someone else is being bad for the image, not because of what they will read in tomorrow's blog, or what they say in the comments. Close your eyes, and when you open them again, you show the world who Tygeria is, and they can take her or leave her. The ones who love you will thank you and still love you. The ones who get mad or afraid or whatever can live with their hate. Because none of that should ever effect that next moment when you go find another quiet spot on top of another building and close your eyes and focus until you are moved to help someone else.

At this point, they are both crying. He's right. She's been doing the right thing but for all the wrong reasons, and it's stressing her out more than she ever knew.

"That's what growing up is," Pa smiles, "learning not to give a damn what anybody else thinks. You do you."

Pa stands up, "I'm not staying for diner; I can't, and you're busy. I just really needed to come say that to you. Why don't you come over at the end of the week we'll do diner at the ranch, and you don't even have to let me know how your week went unless you just want to share it. Because even my opinion of you shouldn't matter."

He heads to the front door and opens it, "Though for the record. No one could be more proud of who you're becoming. I just hate to see fear hold you back."

Tygeria closes the door behind him, takes a deep breath, and drys her eyes. She puts the extra plate back in the cupboard. Then she grabs her plate, makes a sandwich, and sits down on the couch. By the third bite of the sandwich, she tosses the plate on the coffee table, stands up, and heads out the door. She walks around the corner and bolts up into the air, not even switching into her uniform for the first time. It's dark and quiet; there isn't even a breeze tonight. She climbs to 2,000 feet and just floats. She can't just let Tzorion get away with destroying things and taking people. In that, she realizes the anger. She realizes she can't be ruled by anger, but she is. Why give Tzorion that kind of control over her. Pa's right; something has to change.

Tygeria switches into uniform and drops into a free fall then glides north. Falling and then climbing a bit again and falling and climbing. Like swimming through the air, faster and faster till she has crossed more state borders than she knows. Gliding is a workout, no muscles are moving, but there is a tension of the body involved like holding the plank position and still reacting to the air and wind. That and circulating that levitar system that makes her fly gets her heart pumping. She keeps dumping more and more into it, faster and faster. Then she lands in a quiet area near a shopping center. She switches back out of uniform and walks into the market, worn out, and breathing heavily like she just ran a long sprint.

She decides tonight she wants different, so she heads to the camping gear section and grabs a cloth hammock and a bottle of water. She heads to the checkout and pays then, then back out the front door. She checks her phone and realizes she is somewhere in Montana. She walks around to a hidden side of the building and changes into uniform and takes off again. This time she doesn't go far, only about five miles into a state park. She stays away from the official camping area and finds a spot among the trees off in the wilderness. She hangs the hammock and lays there swinging and resting. At first, she figures she will rest before the long trip back home. The night is quiet, and the air is cool but not cold, she ends up falling asleep right there.

The next morning Tygeria wakes up and decides she needs to get back to her city. She rolls up the hammock into its pouch and ties the bag to her belt under her cloak. Then she takes off and points back south. It's daylight, so he glides high enough not to be seen. But curiosity gets the better of her, and she detours through some of the larger cities along the way. About halfway home, she stops in Hyde, deciding she might as well explore and grab some breakfast. She lands quickly behind a building unnoticed, changes back into jeans and t-shirt with a simple thought, and walks around the corner to check out Main Street.

The city is buzzing with activity. People are standing waiting for a bus; others are popping in to buy a bagel at the corner deli. One lady is walking her dog while reading an article on her phone. Tygeria just keeps walking for a while, past bookstores, coffee shops, and cafes. Cars and busses are everywhere, and the sidewalks are full of people in motion. She blends in and matches their pace, quickly heading to nowhere and seeing everything.

Tygeria spots a little grocery store and decides to stop in and find something to eat. She sits at the counter and enjoys a breakfast of eggs and toast. Then she heads back out into the crowd moving once again with the endless flow of people. She spots a library, so she breaks away for a moment and sits on the steps. There are two big stone lions on either end and a tall arched front entryway. Part of her thinks there is too much concrete everywhere, yet she notices that every chance they get, a tree planted or a bush. Every bit of space is used.

She sits there to think through what Pa said the night before. Then she decides if she is doing differently right now. She looks up to the top of the towering buildings around her, then stands and gets back into the flow of people walking. She finds it harder to find a secluded area, but there are side streets and back alleys, so eventually, she quietly takes off into the air and lands on top of the tallest building. She sits down on the corner of the roof, closes her eyes, and enjoys the moment.

After about an hour she catches something, a delivery truck on the freeway has been rear-ended. Except they were on a bridge in the mix-master, and now they are hanging over the edge. Tygeria heads that way and swoops down, landing near the back of the truck so that she doesn't make its balance any worse. Traffic is stopped around them. She opens a sphere and energizes the whole vehicle. Then carefully pulls it backward and sideways onto the road. Once it's placed, she lets go and runs up and opens the driver door.

"You OK?" she asks him.

"Um, yeah," he is stunned and still in shock.

"It's OK; now you won't fall, go ahead and step out of there just to be extra safe," Tygeria tells him.

Then she stands back a bit and holds the door open for him. Motorcycle police are winding their way to the scene through the stopped traffic. The driver takes a second, still rattled, and then steps down out of the delivery truck. Tygeria leaves the driver door open, jogs toward the other side of the bridge, and somersaults over the side then glides away to find the next rescue.

The city is having a quiet morning now as far as accidents go, so Tygeria gets back on track heading home. She liked that last rescue. She didn't do it because she thought she had to, just because she wanted to help someone who needed help. She won't be checking the blog later to see if the remarks are positive or negative because this one won't even be written about. Pa was right; this is the way it should be.

Tygeria makes four more stops on the way home just as she sees people she can help. She doesn't stay to chat, but shes doesn't worry about keeping her distance either. When she gets home, she is so worn out and falls asleep for a while, but content with the day.

Tzorion has finished building his compound. While he still goes out and snatches people as he pleases, he also has to deal with Capitan G to get higher numbers of hostages. This gives him the freedom to experiment more with some of them. He starts trying different formulas and combinations to see if anything else will have the desired effect in a test tube. After all, he is willing to experiment on humans but not on himself. So finding any variations to the treatment or even a cure needs to be lab proven first. In the meantime, he keeps making and taking his usual procedure. Testing in the lab is only frustrating for him, so he decides that he also needs Sanarians to experiment on as well. He starts grooming some of his male prisoners to be the muscle for him. For fear of their own lives, he turns several into soldiers. He works on them for months, making sure they fear to displease him even when he is away. One of these recruits is particularly suited to the task, so Tzorion decides to start training him to take the lead on harvesting and making serum. His name is Pike.

Now that he has Pike leading the compound on Earth, Tzorion gets Capitan G to drop him at Sarani, and he starts building another compound there. He still regularly returns to Earth with Captain G on his runs to mine and load the limestone for him, and the Capitan still resupplies his hostages and discards the bodies. He drops Tzorion back on Sarani before he heads off to meet his buyer; for months, the cycle will continue like that.

Tygeria settles into a pattern as well, and with Tzorion off in another world more often than not, his mayhem and bad press also subside though they do not disappear. He still causes trouble every time he comes back, and the people still live in constant fear of him showing up and destroying things and taking people. No one realizes he regularly leaves, so they don't get to calm down while he is gone.

Tygeria still hangs out with Debbie frequently; they even started going on occasional hikes. Tygeria has stopped calling her for leads, though. She finds those just fine on her own. She is tuned into it more. A call to Debbie is usually just to look up specific information about a building in the moment while she's trying to save someone, but that's it. Debbie still sees it as her mission to spread knowledge and understanding, so she continues the blog almost daily. She noticed Tygeria stopped asking about the comments and replies. So Debbie doesn't talk to Tygeria about the blog anymore.

A few months pass, It is now fall and starting to get cold, especially at night. Tygeria is coming back from a rescue one state over, and in her mind's eye, she picks up on a surge of energy. A transport window has opened somewhere nearby. She finds it, and it's still open. Captain G, Pike, and two others are pushing people off of a charter bus and through the transport window. She quickly heads down, and in the process of landing, she tackles Captain G, and the remaining hostages scatter. She spins around and kicks the captain, and he falls to the ground.

Pike runs over toward Tygeria and throws a few punches then starts beating on her with something called a shock stick. She blocks with her left arm before she fights him off and to the ground. Just as Captain G is about to strike a blow from behind, he gets hit by an unknown figure. This new gentleman pulls open an energy sphere with his right hand and grabs Pike's stick. Then with the snap of his fingers, the shock stick turns to dust along with the shock sticks the others have hanging from their belt. Now that all of them find themselves unarmed, Captain G, Pike, and the two other of Tzorion's soldiers scramble through the transport window and close it behind them. The new guy who was helping, runs after them but just missed getting through the window before it closes.

Tygeria brushes herself off, "Thank you."

"I've been chasing him all over Sarani and Nattur-ial," the stranger says, walking back over to Tygeria. "Sorry, let me start in the right place. My name is Niemia. I am a guardian, and we have observed a lot of your work. You're doing good things here. I think you could help us out. We could certainly give you a hand now and then."

"Interesting, hang on a second," Tygeria says. She walks over and checks on the hostages that escaped, gets them to get back on the bus, tells them to call the police, and stay on the bus because those guys won't come back. Then she heads back over to Niemia.

Niemia is half a foot shorter than she is, male, with blue eyes and brown hair. He keeps his beard short and has a muscular build. He wears a half cloak and a uniform made mostly of thin brown leather. He invites her to follow him, and she does. They head up onto a bluff where they can still see the bus and the people, but they can talk in private.

"Go ahead and ask," Niemia says. "You seem to be taking this well; you're not afraid of me?"

"Should I be?" Tygeria asks.

"No," he laughs and sits down in the grass.

She sits down beside him,

"You're not from around here," Tygeria says.

He laughs, "No, I'm not. I am from a planet called Avalon and invited into the guardianship about ten years ago. They saw my work on Avalon and wanted to offer me the tools and support to keep helping but on several worlds. It comes in handy when you start encountering evil people that jump around on several planets. We also help with trouble and disasters on several planets, plus we can chase down the big troublemakers. I've been tracking the Captain and Tzorion for months now, but I can't find their main base of operations, so they keep getting away."

"You have bioenergy like me," Tygeria says.

"Yes, most of my people do, and most Sanarians do, which is how you have it," Niemia explains. "That said, almost none of them have this much that they can channel and use the excess. Not only that, but guardians also use something we call a guardian cuff."

He shows her a metal coil twisted around his upper right arm. "You have a set amount of extra bioenergy when you max out at that's all you have to use. Once you use most of it up, your body makes more until you hit that set point again. This cuff can store excess energy you can tap into. You back build your energy into it, and your body will make more. That way, in a fight, you can use everything you've got, instead of having to wait two or three hours to charge back up. Then you can draw from the cuff and fully reload. It would help you handle the big stuff. I was like you struggling with the airplane earlier this year."

"If you saw that, why didn't you come help?" Tygeria asks as gently as possible, trying not to accuse him, really just wondering.

"I'm a bit jealous," Niemia says. "You see, I'm not a flier. I can use my guardian tower to drop down on to a planet at any specific point and then go back up into the tower, but I can't just fly along beside a plane like you do."

"Guardian tower?" Tygeria asks.

"In orbit around each populated planet in the known universe, about 15 total. There are a few unclaimed, but they are all linked together. They are invisible and shielded. We moved the one for Earth into a slightly different orbit about a year ago because it looked likely to be in the path of Earth's new space program. It's in a good safe spot now, no worries." Niemia says.

"I blew your mind, didn't I," Niemia says. Well, since we have finally officially run into each other, I would like to offer you a guardian cuff, and you can just think about if you want to start helping a larger portion of your planet and maybe even one day keep an eye on Sarani too."

He excuses himself and stands up, steps a few feet away, and then with a bit of a jump, he disappears into a swirl of purple energy that shoots up into the sky. When he returns minutes later, the purple light shoots back down, and with a swirl of light, he jumps to the ground. He is holding an extra energy cuff.

"Here, just try it out for a while," Niemia hands her the cuff, and she puts it on her upper right arm.

He talks her through the process of closing her eyes and focusing her energy into the cuff. "Come on, let's try it out. Meet me here; it's an unused warehouse. Niemia uses the tower to change locations quickly, and Tygeria glides over at top speed, it's only 10 minutes away. Inside, she walks over to a heavy pallet of goods and energizes it, then floats above it and picks it up. Then she sets it down and walks over to the wall.

"Wow," Tygeria says, "with this much energy, forget lighting up a room."

She touches the wall, and every wall in every room has a light glow that lights the room. She gasps her mind racing through the possibilities. "I could dust an entire building. Oh no. I would never want to do that. Heaven forbid I should ever need to. If I dusted the building, no one would have been crushed, but they all would have dropped, and the fall would have killed them all."

"No," Niemia snaps. "Don't do that. Don't go there. Never second guess a rescue from the past. I've seen that literally drive guardians mad."

"But is it not smart to think through better ways to do things so we can do better the next time?" Tygeria points out.

"Sure," Niemia says. "But always pick a new building, a new place. Look at that one and play the what-if game. Just don't ever second guess past rescues. You did your best, and it makes a difference, and you move on to the next. You don't strike me as one that has a lot of regrets despite a long list of rescues. But just then, I know the look, there is one that haunts you."

"Yeah, a building collapse, I was convinced I didn't rescue a single person," Tygeria says. "In fact, I think the only reason that it is the one that haunts me is because it was the only time I got trapped myself. I had to lay there and wait to be rescued. And they tried, they were coming for me. I ended up getting some strength back and meeting them halfway."

"OK," Niemia turns to her very seriously, "I'm gonna help you with this one. I want you to close your eyes and just imagine you can go back in time just before you even entered this building you're thinking of. You're just floating there in front of it. Everything is going to happen the same way except you're on the outside facing a decision, you know the future, the building still falls, the people who die still die and I have just one question for you. Do you still go in? Knowing you will survive just as you did. What changes if you don't even go in?"

Tygeria sit's there with her eyes closed and thinks it through. The people she saw for the last time in the final moments of their life.

"Would you still go in, or do you stand there and watch it happen from the outside?" Niemia says.

"Yes," Tygeria says, "yes, I go in."

"Why?" he asks, not out of confusion but leading her through the thought process.

"They were so happy in that last moment," Tygeria says, she pictures a dozen hopeful faces that she helped them move to the exits and the group that was trapped in the room until she let them out. They were energized and optimistic. "They were so afraid before I came in, I can't imagine them continuing through that fear through the moment they were... I'd rather give them the moment of hope even if they still die ten minutes later."

"Because you made a difference," Niemia points out, "you just didn't get the outcome you wanted, but you made a difference."

"Thanks," Tygeria says.

"Any time," he stands up and dusts himself off. "We will no doubt, meet again soon. I keep helping out on Earth, but since you have been pretty active, I've mainly just handled the stuff happening in Europe, etc. I will continue to do so."

"By the way, now you have enough energy, you could land an airplane." Niemia smiles, then he takes off back up into the guardian tower.

Tygeria spends the rest of the night experimenting with how much energy she has and how much she can do at once. Eventually, she wears herself out and uses it all up, so she goes home to her apartment to rest. She thinks she likes the cuff; it's new, it's different. She doesn't completely trust it yet, so she takes it off her arm and sets it on the nightstand by her bed. She just doesn't think to take it with her when she leaves the next day.

That afternoon Tygeria and Debbie are watching one of Debbie's favorite shows. "I'm sorry, but if you're running from Zombies, you're not gonna stop and grab a leaf blower, that's not a weapon," Debbie says.

"Well," Tygeria says, "I bet that means they are about to kill off Zack."

"They wouldn't dare," Debbie says as Zack suddenly gets killed off in the show.

"That's it," Debbie says, turning off the TV. "I'm no longer a fan if they aren't keeping Zack."

"Of course they are keeping him, now he just has to play a zombie," Tygeria points out. "OK, I'm too restless, I'm gonna go find a cat stuck in a tree at least."

"Oh, yes!" Debbie laughs, "looking forward to writing that blog."

"Don't you dare," Tygeria says, stepping into the backyard. She changes into uniform and takes off. She didn't bring the cuff and hasn't told anybody, not Pa nor Debbie, that she met Niemia the other day. She is still trying to process life on a universal scale herself.

Tygeria glides way above the streets and neighborhoods of Worth. Everything looks calm and normal, but for a few rain clouds rolling in. Thirty minutes later, gliding is wearing her out, and the rain has started to fall. It's just a gentle light rain, but collectively she is beginning to get wet. She realizes she is near the mall and figures she can go inside for a while until the storm clears. It's busy there. A lot of people decided to head into the mall since the rain started. She finds a clear spot to land on the far side of a parking garage.

She has an eerie feeling that someone is behind her. She remembers that Niemia has apparently been watching her patrols. Is he following her to see if she's using the cuff? That is the first moment she realizes she didn't bring the cuff to experiment with some more. Then, sure enough, she catches the sense of an energy being coming up behind her very quickly. As she turns to look, she feels a hard hit to her head, and then her whole body is tightened up from an electrical shock. This is apparently what a shock stick feels like. Tzorion knocks her out cold before she even saw him coming.

He doesn't take her to the compound he built on Earth. Capitan G is there in the background with a window open to his ship in orbit. Tzorion scoops her up, and they step through the window. Captain G drops them off at Tzorion's newer compound on Sarani. He mostly has humans there. He has started experimenting on Sanarians now too, and after a while, he cages them on the Earth compound. This way, even if any of his hostages were to escape, they would still be stuck on the wrong planet.

Episode 8

Tygeria wakes up with a splitting headache. She is lying on her side. Her head hurts, and her ears are ringing. She is in a room that is dimly lit. She closes her eyes and reads the faint energy coming off the objects and walls. It's a large room, no furniture, and the bright, loud energy of several other people off to the side of the room. She can barely see. Someone on the other side of the room is crying, and the whole place smells like mildew. It's cold. Much colder than outside. Almost cold enough to make everyone shiver, but not quite.

Tygeria's heart is pounding. She sits up and leans against the wall. She touches the wall and fills it with energy; this lets her read more of the layout of the whole building. It's huge. There are lots of soldiers, and she can tell Tzorion is in a room with other people several rooms away. It's a single-story building, but it's almost the size of a city block. It's out in a secluded forest area.

The whole place is made of metal and concrete. There is a bathroom in the corner and several buckets around with ladles in some of them. It turns out one is filled with drinking water, and one is filled with oatmeal; the others are empty earlier versions of oatmeal buckets that have been eaten already.

"Hi, my name is Kate," one of the other hostages starts walking towards her. Aside from the fact that we have all been abducted by aliens. Are you OK? I can show you around the room, but it won't take long."

"The name is Tygeria," Tygeria says.

"I'm gonna have to get you to write that one down one day," Kate laughs. "Do you need some water?"

"No, I'm fine," Tygeria says, "but thank you. How long have you been here?"

Kate sits down and leans up against the wall beside her. "About two weeks now," Kate says. Dave has been here the longest—three months. He's an insurance guy; I'm a teacher. The guy in the red shirt over there is the Scott; he works as a Hollywood cameraman. Bobby is the guy in the Rangers baseball cap he works in construction. So far, it seems we are from all different states, different kinds of jobs. The only thing we have in common is we were tricked into thinking we hit someone on the road and pulled over only to get knocked out and dragged here. The two over there in the corner, Christy and Rebecca, were in the same car, but they are the only two that already knew each other."

"Why are we here?" Tygeria asks her.

"Not sure," Kate says, "all I know is about every other day one or two people are taken out of here, and they never come back."

"Someones coming," Tygeria tells Kate, and then she scrambles to her feet.

The door opens, and Tzorion comes in. He walks straight over to her, and hand to chest slams her against the wall. "Well, well, well, we finally meet," Tzorion says. "I've seen you all over the news. You're like me; we should work together."

"Not if this is your kinda work," Tygeria says.

Tzorion opens an energy sphere with his right hand and fills it with fire. Then he holds it right beside her face.

"Are you afraid?" Tzorion asks.

"No," she says, deciding not to give him the satisfaction of bullying her.

"That's nice; you will be," Tzorion says, then he throws her to the ground. He starts swinging at her, so she ducks and dodges over and over again. Then he pulls out a shock stick and starts pounding her shoulder, full force, each hit causing light electrical burns that just compound on each other. Her shoulder is throbbing; she tenses up and braces for each impact. Then he stops, and she cries out in pain, trembling, consumed by the pain, she has no strength left to strike back. He leans in and whispers in her ear, "I win."

Then he turns and walks toward the door signaling to his guards. They grab one more person to take out with them, and then they all leave. Tygeria drops to the floor, still tense from the pain and tries to breathe through it and calm down. Thinking to herself, He wins, huh, don't give him the satisfaction of making you scream. Never again.

"You OK?" Kate rushes back over to her, "that's odd. They mainly leave us alone except the one person they drag out of here. Even when Bobby started hitting one of the soldiers, they never hit back, they just pushed him away and kept doing their thing. I wonder why he actually came in here and just started beating on you."

Pike and Tzorion are in another room that has been set up as a lab. They strap their hostage to a table and sit down at a counter along the side of the room.

"So, what are you going to do with her?" Pike asks him.

"Who, Tygeria?" Tzorion asks.

"Yeah," Pike says. "You want me to kill her, so she doesn't give us trouble? I can tell just looking at her that she's is not going to cooperate."

"No," Tzorion says, "I'm looking forward to breaking her."

"What do you mean by break? Surly not useless and drooling kind of broken." Pike says.

"I want her standing behind me completely loyal, handling my dirty work for me. In fact, we need someone who can take over-harvesting and keeping all those terrible humans in line. I need you free for the fuel manufacture and sales end of things," Tzorion explains. "I need her afraid of me; it's a delicate science because I still need her strong too. It will take time, but we have plenty of that."

"Next time you go in there, get her to do something you demand," Tzorion tells Pike. "Get her to pick the next person we harvest for my treatment. In fact, I want time to figure out why she doesn't seem to be having the same problem that I have. There's a chance she might be my cure."

Tygeria gives her shoulder time to stop hurting, and then she starts exploring the room. Her first thought is to dust the door. She lays her hand against the door, and it feels strange. She tries to feed her energy into it, but something has been done the energy won't stay. They have done something to the doors

and walls that resist bioenergy. A week passes before anyone enters the room again. The group gets to
know each other and lives off the drinking water and
cold oatmeal. They all ask Tygeria if any of her little
save the world tricks can do them any good in here.
She assures them she will do everything she can, but
she is just as stuck as they are. Just as the bucket of oatmeal starts getting low, Pike comes in and sets down
another one. He says nothing, he touches nothing, and
then he leaves.

Tzorion comes in later that week, walks right over
to Tygeria while everyone, including her, are sound
asleep on the floor, and he uses a shock stick to the
back to wake her up, then pins her to the wall.

"You're going to do something for me," Tzorion
says in her ear.

"I need one of them so I can do my treatment,"
Tzorion holds the back of her neck and pulls her up
and points her toward the main group of people. "You
pick, which one do I kill and harvest next?"

"Pick me," Tygeria replies in a gruff, angry, even
defiant voice.

"No no no, that's not how this works," Tzorion
gives a sinister chuckle, "it needs to be 100% human,
there's only one teenie tiny organ that is the key ingredient that finishes the formula that keeps me alive.
You're a muddy mess of two species, and I'm not get-

ting anywhere near that kind of poison. Which one you pick." He drags her closer.

"Me," she says, fear in her voice but not in her eyes as she looks directly into his eyes, angry.

"Yea, playing it that way. That's fine."

He punches her hard in the side and throws her down. Then his guys grab someone near the door and head out. Tygeria scrambles to her feet, clutching her sore rib cage and rushes toward them only to slam sideways into the closing cage door. Shouting in pain, she calms down and forces herself to take some slow deep breaths.

"Thank you," Kate says from the corner.

Tzorion comes back in five hours later and rushes Tygeria and starts kicking her, then drops a shock stick in front of her.

"You wanna fight, let's fight," Tzorion growls, then he shifts backward and stands ready, one foot back one foot forward weapon arm back ready to strike, but he wants her to move first. This has to be a trap she thinks; he's giving me a weapon. I need to defeat him. I would be foolish not to take a weapon and use it. She takes a deep breath and then picks up the shock stick. He rushes her the minute she touches it. Tygeria tries to block, but he does four rapid hits, and she manages to block the first and the last. The others leave a combination burn and bruise on her arm and side. Stunned, she's slower, and he strikes another blow across the face and head, and she drops. He removes the shock stick from her hand and leaves, taking no one, saying nothing.

Tygeria pondered the advantage of attack vs. defend. How should she handle this?

The group is starting to talk to her more, how can we help? We can't fight him at all. We know we need you. Thank you for being so determined to protect us, how can we help? Spread out and stay away from the door just to give me more time when I'm dealing with him.

"Do you also require these treatments that he's doing? Are you guys the same?" Kate asks.

"Only that we are both Sanarian and human hybrids," Tygeria answers. "As I understand it, he has a birth defect that keeps trying to kill him, and he found an odd, horrid solution for it. So no, I'm good just as I am. My only requirement so far is that I have to at least float regularly, which is why I sleep over the floor sometimes instead of on it."

"That's good," Kate says.

"Gee, if I could float instead of sleeping on this hard, messy, cold metal floor, I would do that every night," Kate says.

"Well, I tend always to start that way, and it tapers off as I sleep apparently," Tygeria smiles.

"Do you sleep that way at home, floating every night?" someone else asks.

"No, usually gliding does the trick, a powerful climb thousands of feet into the air, adrenaline pumping, levitar at max circulation, and I'm good for a week," Tygeria says.

"Levitar? That's that clear fluid that Sanarians have that runs parallel to your circulatory system, and it circulates and stores bioenergy," they ask.

"Yes," Tygeria answers.

"So the news about the Sanarians we are working on meeting up with, can they fly too, like you?" they ask.

"No, they only have five percent of the energy I do, and it subconsciously adjusts to the different gravity pressure extremes on parts of their planet," Tygeria explains. "At least according to one well-traveled gentleman I met once. As Tzorion said, I'm the mess of two species, and this is my resulting flaw. Not a bad flaw since I learned to control it, and getting better every day."

"Neat. Sorry, I hope it doesn't feel like we're grilling you, we're just trying to understand," Kate says.

"I'll answer anything I can, I don't have all the answers, but I believe the more any two people know about each other, the better. Knowledge defeats fear," Tygeria says.

"Deep but yes, a good point," Kate says.

Another week passes before Tzorion comes in again. "Kneel to me, and I will only take one instead of two," he tells Tygeria.

"No," Tygeria says.

His guards grab two more hostages. Tygeria starts to kneel, but instead, she springs across the room in a half gliding jump and smashes into one of the guards. Then she kicks his legs out from under him. Then she grabs the other guard by the back of his collar and throws him over her back, flying up into the ceiling at the same time, and he smashes against the ceiling then drops to the floor. The guards run out of the room, deciding Tzorion needs to handle this level of trouble. He just looks at her then calmly walks out alone.

Tygeria stands quickly any time the door opens. Any time they come in, she is determined to stand in the gap. She puts herself between the others and the soldiers. Over and over again, sometimes they beat her down and take a hostage anyway, and sometimes she fights well enough to stop them. They have shock sticks and use them often. Tygeria resolves not to give them the satisfaction of screaming in pain; she tries to duck and dodge quicker.

A few weeks pass. Tygeria wakes up, and her heart starts pounding. Almost before her eyes open, she flips from the sleeping position onto her hands and knees, ready to strike, ready to block, ready to jump, find the people first, don't hurt them—all within seconds. Then the room comes into focus. Both visually, tho it's dark, and in her mind's eye. The read she gets off the bioenergy aura that gives her a clearer, more in-depth focus on the room. Where is he, where are they? This becomes ingrained, so deeply, she almost isn't fully awake yet. Ask her a question as she is flipping over and scanning, she won't even hear it, yet it's becoming a habit of survival.

A week later, the soliders and Captin G brings in seven new people, bound, gagged, and thrown against the wall. Once the soldiers leave, the group carefully unties the new hostages and introduce themselves. The days turn into weeks; the faces keep changing. Tygeria keeps taking short naps so she can be awake to protect them.

Tzorion comes in. The whole room is asleep again; he walks over to Tygeria and starts poking a shock stick in her back. Tygeria starts to wake up, her heart starts pounding, eyes not even open yet, she flips over and jumps out of his reach to the middle of the room, she scans the room, ready to strike or block, find the people, where are they, where is he? Protect them, can't strike out, can't hurt the people—heart pounding. Wake up. Breathe. He comes at her again she tries to get the shock stick away from him so she will have something to hit with. But she can't get it from him.

He keeps torturing her, and Tygeria has decided to use him as practice, practice to become a better fighter. When he's not there, she starts trying to come up with new moves and then practices them over and over again so that she can execute them quickly. She practices on him and his soldiers, gradually getting better at fighting. She gets to the point that every time they come in, they leave empty-handed, even Tzorion. She stands in the gap over and over again.

The soldiers are settling into a pattern, and Tzorion himself comes less and less. He happens to be spending a lot of time at the other compound experimenting on Sanarians.

Over and over again, like clockwork. Today she finds a spot in the ceiling that has an electrical box behind the ceiling tile. She starts messing with the box. After thirty minutes of experimenting with the box, she turns it off. Turns what off she's not sure but happy to turn anything off in this place, convinced everyone would be better if nothing worked. She jumps back down and tries to see what has changed. Out of habit, she touches the wall to energize it, and now it actually works. That box was protecting the walls from bioenergy, but now…

She quietly wakes the others and lets them know she has a way out, get ready, and stay quiet. One of them named Susan helps wake the rest and fill them in. She tells Tygeria to start leading them out. Tygeria heads to the back corner of the room and energizes the wall, then in a very controlled action she draws most of the power back until there is just a large spot of wall glowing, she dusts it. There is a hall on the other side, they step through, and she touches the wall of the hallway, now she can get a read on the entire complex, The whole place is asleep except for them. Quickly and quietly, she leads them to the most direct way out of the building.

It is night as they emerge from the building. She breathes a sigh of relief, knowing the dark will protect a bit. Yet it is brighter than expected. Then at the same time, several notice why. Not only is there a full moon tonight, but there are also two.

"Were not on Earth anymore, are we," Susan says. "Where are we?"

"I think it's the woods of Sarani."

"Isn't that supposed to be dangerous gravity or something?" Susan asks.

"Not as long as we don't have to go far," Tygeria explains. "Logically, the gate they brought us through is close by; we shouldn't have to travel far enough to get into a gravity pocket, and clearly, we are not in one here."

"Oh, okay," Susan says, "I'm sure you'll tell us if we get close to one."

"I didn't know their gravity was different here?" Mike says as they all start walking toward the tree line.

"Well yeah, the main difference between a Human and a Sanarian is that Levitar system that adjusts automatically as they walk through pockets of extreme gravity caused by the two moons," Susan explains proudly, "that's how Tygeria can fly, she is the unique feature of being able to not only control that effect but also magnify it to extremes."

"You've been researching or something?" Mike asks Susan.

"I've kept up with all the different things Earth Central has released about what they've learned so far," Susan smiles, "it's all so fascinating, isn't it."

"I just wanna get home," someone from the back of the group adds.

"Working on that. " Tygeria reassures the group.

They head into the woods, grateful that they still go unnoticed, no one chasing them. The thick forest gives them even better cover. As the group breaks through the tree line into the densely wooded area, Tygeria bends down and picks up a tall stick. She brushes the fallen leaves and grass off and then wraps her right hand tightly around it near the top. She clos-es her eyes and visualizes her bioenergy radiating out from her and filling the stick. The group watches as the stick slowly starts to glow blue light; eventually, it's bright enough to see the trees for 10 feet. That's not the point, though.

Eyes still closed she forcefully taps the bottom end of the stick against the ground four times in a row. Each time it dims in brightness further and further un-til it's back to being just a stick. But the light that was in it rushes along the ground radiating out in large circles for miles. By the last tap, the radius has satu-rated the ground for 10 miles. It's not enough energy to light the ground, it's more like dropping a stone in a pool of water, and there is a dimly lit circle rushing away bigger and bigger.

The point on this is not light. As the energy radiates out, Tygeria gets a detailed look at the surroundings. Her eyes are still closed, and she already knows that within a ten-mile radius, there are 15 people besides her, two foxes, eight squirrels, and one creek. She can also see the gate. The energy of it stands out in her mind's eye.

She opens her eyes and points west, "the gate home is eight miles that way."

They are all quietly gathered around and attentive after seeing what her energy can do. Most are confident they are the safest following her lead. She's able to tell where to go, and she kept standing in the gap protecting them. At this point, trust is strong even if most are not comfortable talking to her or asking her questions just because she's the alien.

"We will have to walk by moonlight, so just go slow and watch your step," Tygeria starts walking through the trees toward the distant creek. "I can kinda see where you guys are behind me; if we get too spread out, I'll stop, and we can gather up again. If the people at the back of the group get too far back, I won't be able to see them anymore."

"We're with you," several of the members of the group say, they are all starting to get more comfortable.

The group hesitates to talk very loud, still worried about getting recaptured. They keep an eye on each other and walk carefully through the woods. Tygeria hangs on to the stick, adopting it as a staff weapon and uses it as a hiking stick to help climb up the steep inclines, etc. Several others in the group know a good idea when they see one and search the ground for a good hiking stick for themselves. It takes a couple of hours to get to the creek through the thick trees and steep climbs and drops.

The creek isn't too bad, but it's pretty broad. Once again, Tygeria taps her staff on the group four times.

This one isn't for very much information, so she doesn't have to close her eyes and focus. "The creek is three feet at its deepest, but that's 22 feet across, so go slow and carefully."

"Can you to that trick and freeze it so we can just walk across the top? mike asks.

"Did you bring your ice skates?" Tygeria says, "that current wouldn't make it stable anyway. Sorry."

"No, you're fine, just a thought," Mike says.

"I don't know about you guys, but I haven't had a bath in months; I'm looking forward to this," Susan says, running toward the creek. Several members of the group laugh and agree.

Can we drink it? " one of them asks.

"I can get us some cleaner water than that once we get to the gate," Tygeria assures him.

They all carefully make their way into the water, trying to follow single file, so they don't step in a hole. Many of them dunk down and scrub their hair for a second and then rub their arms and clothes in the running water. They each emerge on the other side and wait for the others. It's a slightly warm evening so the wet clothes are pleasant and will dry within the hour. The weather is about 78 though it is early in the night, and the temperature will continue to drop as they get closer to midnight. At this pace, they will reach their destination by then.

Tygeria waits until everyone is across, and she crosses last. Then once again, they disappear into the tree line, hiking the remaining three miles to the gate. The trees are filled with birds and insects chirping. The air smells fresh and clean with a slight hint of damp wood. Thankfully the moonlight is so bright they can see the ground below them to watch their step. Tygeria retakes the lead, and everyone keeps close to the person in front of them so they can all stay on the trail.

They approach the pillar for the gate that played a part in getting them here.

"How do we turn it on? Can only he do it?" Susan asks Tygeria.

"We can do the same way he does. One of the Gate Activators is here so I can turn it on. We just have to wait for a cycle," Tygeria says. "I wonder if Sarani Central knows this one is here? Actually, I wonder if he built it himself for his own use?" She uses her bioenergy to charge up the Activator, and it shows a countdown until the next time the alignment will open the gate to Earth.

Tygeria triggers the Activator and places it into the port marked for Earth Central. As she does this, she notices an extra port marked on this piler that none of the others have had. She wonders for a moment where that one would lead. The activator counts down the wormhole alignment as three hours away.

"We have three hours to kill guys, so just stay right here near the pillar, and I will go get us some water," Tygeria says.

"We will get some firewood!" two of the guys pipe up, and they start picking up fallen branches off the ground.

The pillar is in a clearing without tree coverage, not so big that they feel out in the open but enough that Tygeria can take off into the cool night sky a few hundred feet up. She spots the lake that the creek feeds into 50 miles away and drops down into a high-speed glide. She is there in ten minutes. She opens a sphere of energy and throws it into the water. She heats the sphere, so the water around it is boiling and sterilized and then quickly freezes a section that's about the size of a wrecking ball. Then she jumps back up into the air pulling the large frozen ball of clean water out of the lake, and it follows her as she glides back to camp.

When she gets back, the guys have already managed to light the fire, and everyone is around it drying off. She carefully sets the giant sphere of ice right on the ground.

"The outer two inches worth are dirty, but the inside layers have been boiled clean," Tygeria tells the group.

Then she opens an energy sphere again and pushes it inside the big ball of ice until it is centered. She heats it slowly so the inner layers of ice melt into the water, but the outer layers remain to contain it. Then she burns a hole in the upper side to access the water.

"Make your own cup and dig in," Tygeria says to the group.

The group laughs and thanks her, then some of them set out to find leaves while others enjoy the warm fire and rest after the long walk. Tygeria heads over and leans up against a nearby tree, exhausted from the day. They still have over two hours on the countdown, but then they can step through right into the Earth Central holding area courtyard. An hour and a half pass, and the ice ball melts down to half it's size. The men are enjoying playing with the fire enough that they keep feeding it fresh wood. It's actually twice as big as the first version.

Then, in Tygeria's mind eye, she picks up on some activity back at the compound. She jumps to her feet, taps her stick for a more precise look. They have discovered the room is empty and scrambling to figure out where the location of the group. They check all the doors and find them to be locked, so they keep searching inside the building. Tygeria sits back down.

"Everything okay?" Susan asks.

"Yep," Tygeria answers.

She doesn't want to worry them needlessly. They have all been through enough these last six months.

Tygeria nervously keeps track of the building, looking for any of the soldiers to come outside. Twenty minutes later, ten of Tzorion's soldiers leave the building. They stop and talk a minute and then start running into the woods. They know where the gate is and assume the hostages desire to go home, so they head straight for the gate.

"Guys, it's okay, but I can tell the soldiers are looking for us, just FYI. They know we've left, and they are starting to walk around outside." Tygeria tells the group.

"Dang, I wish this thing would activate already. Can we speed it up?" Mike asks.

"It's waiting for an interstellar alignment to happen that helps you travel hundreds of light-years across space in an instant, so no. We are pretty much at its mercy." Tygeria explains. "Don't worry; they won't get here in time. We will get home tonight."

Three of the soldiers are getting close, running directly to the gate with good strong lights and a sold knowledge of the path. They are getting there faster than she wants.

"I'm gonna go slow them down, as soon as it opens all of you just go."

"You need to come with us!" Susan insists.

"I will. I can move faster than you can, don't wait for me."

The clock keeps ticking closer to the time the gate will open, and once it hits the twenty-minute mark, many members of the group stand, restless and excited. Tzorion's soldiers are getting close. Tygeria tightens up in fear.

Tygeria heads away from the camp and the light of the fire, halfway back to the soldiers. She uses her energy to thinly cut through a few trees and push them over to block the path. Then she heads back to the group. The gate has opened, and they are scrambling through into the welcome sight of officers at Earth Central. Tygeria is within ten feet of the open gate. Everyone else is through when she is tackled from behind by one of Tzorion's soldiers.

She turns and starts kicking him, trying to scramble free. He grabs a log out of the nearby fire and hits her over the head. By then, two other soldiers have run into the clearing as well. The soldiers at Earth Central see this and see that Tygeria isn't moving. They can't run back through the gate because you can only travel one way at a time, so they cut the connection to prevent the soldiers from running through.

All his prisoners are gone.

They chase her down through the woods, the group makes it back to earth, but she holds off Tzorion instead of making it through.

Tygeria realizes she is caged again; her heart starts pounding, eyes not even open yet, she flips over, scans the room, ready to strike or block, ready to jump away from a strike, find the people, where are they, where is he? Protect them, can't strike out, can't hurt the people. She sits in the empty room. It's a different one than the previous room. She figures she will wait until they go to sleep, and then she will destroy the box in the ceiling and leave.

Tzorion is standing over her, she tries to react and jump across the room, but she can't move, something has already happened. Then the pain sets in. It creeps up and rises and rises. Her leg her entire leg, the pain is blinding. Before she was even awake, before she could sense that he entered, Tzorion came in so quickly and brought an ax down on her leg, right below the knee. He strikes again before she can get her bearings. He cuts clean through. A few of his helpers are in the room now, too; she doesn't even notice them. The pain is blinding; she thinks she is screaming, but she can't hear herself. Then blackness. She's out.

Tzorion has his workers pick her up and carry her to a room that has a clean bed prepped. He planned for this. He brought in a doctor who handles the wound. He wants to break her spirit, not kill her. He wants to take her leg and her spirit and her spunk, but not her life. So he prepared and left to sleep in an actual bed.

The doctor tends the wound and bandages for several days.

The doctor kept her sedated so she wouldn't wake up and give anyone any trouble. He needed her to have time to heal and be stable so he could adequately start messing with her again. So he left her alone with the doctor for a few weeks. Then he returned her to the big empty room and left her alone so the drugs could wear off. Returned to her cage, in the dark, in the quiet.

Tygeria starts to wake up. Her heart starts pounding, eyes not even open yet, she rolls over slightly, unable to flip over. She realizes she is alone. She remembers the pain, and in a panic, her hand moves down and feels her right knee, it's sore and then nothing below it. Her stomach drops. Then she remembers the pain. Almost like it was the last second in her life before this one. Like she just woke from a nightmare.

"No," she shouts into the big empty.

The room echos. "No, you will not break me!!! Cut every Dang piece off! I will never help you. I will never tolerate you! I will never come! I will never pick it up!' she screams at the top of her lungs into the emptiness. "No!"

She worries. How does she keep fighting this? How does she win? She got the people out, that's a win. He will just collect more. How does she win, she needs to get out. How does she get out, she needs to survive. She still wins as long as she survives.

She lets her head drop down to the floor and passes out again and sleeps for days. When she wakes, the compound is quiet; it's the middle of the night. She tosses a sphere up to the ceiling panel and sets it on fire, destroying the box. Then crawling over to the main door, she dusts the door into the room and unable to stand, crawls down the hallway, and out of the complex. This time she takes off into the sky and glides away from the compound straight to the window in the woods and glides through to Earth.

Episode 9

Tygeria feels lost. She doesn't want to land; her leg aches terribly. She is malnourished, dehydrated, and it's been so long since she flew last that she feels heavy and can barely go higher than a typical skyscraper. No phone wallet or keys. She knows she needs to figure out her location before she can dream of pointing toward home. Fortunately, it's night, so being closer to the ground doesn't risk being spotted. She passes over a shopping center and can tell by the stores that she is in the right country. But what state is she in so she can head to Texas.

She spotted a large city in the distance, and she got close enough to a cluster of hotels off the Interstate Highway to see the names on the sign. Kansas City near I-35. She climbs up but glides parallel to I-35, knowing it will take her right home.

It had been more than a year. What time is it? Will Ma and Pa even be awake? She's probably lost her apartment after that much time. She decides none of that matters. She just desperately needs a soft bed and a hot meal.

There it is—home. A streetlight illuminates the front section of the driveway. A light on at the peak of the barn door also provides visibility. She tumbled to the ground in a one-legged attempt to land in the grass just a few feet from the back deck. Trying to sit up in the grass so she can call for Pa, her energy leaves her. It's been such a long day, and at this point, she can't even persuade herself to sit up. So she lays there on her side in the fresh green grass and allows her heavy eyelids to close.

Fortunately, Pa saw something out of the corner of his eye. He had taken up the habit of sitting in the open-air section of the living room. It was spring, so there was no fire in the fireplace. He had the lights off. Ma was upstairs in the family room watching the news. Pa just sits there in the dark, seeing the world as it is in the moonlight.

He catches a shadow out of the corner of his eye, and something compels him to check it out this time. The minute he stands and turns, he sees a person lying on their side passed out in the yard. He's too far away, and there's too little light to tell it's his daughter. But a knot forms in the pit of his stomach anyway, just an instinct he knows it's her...finally. He shouts in a panic upstairs at Ma to come quick and then as if there were no furniture or railings in the way he leaps from his recliner to the yard, rushing to Tygeria's side.

"Tyger," he says as he gets close, "thank goodness."

But then he cuts the sentence off as if the words and even his very breath are snatched from him. He sees that her right leg is missing below the knee. Her stump is still bruised and bloodied looking and then nothing. It takes him a minute to comprehend what he sees.

"It's OK, I've got ya," he says.

Tygeria is still out cold. Pa tries to wrap his head around what she must have lived through. He gently picks her up, realizing how light and thin she's become. He carriers her steady and gently back up to and into the house as his mind starts taking note of more signs of long term torture.

Ma is waiting breathlessly on the deck. Pa gets her inside.

Ma gets her cleaned up, and into fresh clothes, they didn't recognize her. They keep doubting it's their daughter because she looks so different. Is it really her? This random person is lying in the yard, skin and bone. She looks so fragile and thin they are afraid to touch her. However, she wasn't that fragile.

Tygeria was still out cold when Mark arrives. He scrambles over to where they have her on the couch. He is breathless and stunned as he checks what he can. Blood pressure, temperature, clearly malnourished and dehydrated.

Upon hearing that, Ma heads into the kitchen and to make tea.

"What would she eat?" she asks.

"Start with something mild, oatmeal, mashed potatoes, something like that, something easy to digest," Mark suggests.

When the other survivors came back, they said they were fed porridge for almost a year—porridge in water. It might be hard to digest too much else at first. Then he focuses on his biggest concern, cleaning her leg. He checks where she was scarred instead of sutured. It's swollen and bruised, but he realizes it has healed a lot and technically stable, just needs a little love. An ice pack, and we can see about fitting her for a prosthetic leg once she has gotten her strength back.

Tygeria starts to wake up. Her heart begins pounding. Her eyes not open yet, she flips over, scans the room, ready to strike or block, ready to jump away from a strike, find the people, where are they, where is he? Protect them, can't strike out, can't hurt the people. Heart pounding. Wake up. Breathe. What room? This is different. She springs from the couch to the wall behind the couch. She is on the floor, not accustomed to all the obstacles. Furniture is in the way everywhere. It's not the cage. She blinks and tries to focus. How is it not the cage?

Mark fell backward, completely startled at the sudden movement. Pa reacted by jumping out of his chair to his feet. He started to walk toward her, but Mark puts his hand up to stop him.

"It's OK; you're safe. You're home." Pa says in a calm tone, deliberately trying to relax her, even though he's nervous.

What has she been through, how has it changed her?

"It just me, Mark, trying to help you out. It's only me, your folks here. You're fine," Mark spoke deliberately and calmly. Even purposefully turning his back to her as he spoke, picking up a few tools he knocked over when he fell back.

"You look like you've been to hell and back," Mark continues. "Several other survivors made it back about a month ago, and they were talking about how much you helped them. So we know a little about where you guys were and how you were treated."

Mark nods at Pa, and eagerly, but restrained, stands and walks over to Tygeria and kneels in front of her.

"Can you come back over to the couch?" he asks.

She smiles and puts her hand on his shoulder just for the warm touch. Then she gets her focus and remembers she got home, this is home, this is the living room. This is family.

She takes a deep breath and focuses on Pa beside her. She calms down, picks a chair to target, and gently guides Pa to step sideways out of the way. He was trying to figure out the best way to pick her up or help her get to the chair, but then she springs back over to the couch and uses it to rest her short leg on and walks a few steps along the couch, then drops down into the comfy recliner at the end.

"Well, I can see you've already started to adapt, but I will bring you some crutches in the morning so you can get around better." Mark grins.

"Are you talking to me yet?" she just gives him a tired smile. "No rush, take you time. How about some food first?"

Ma is now standing behind them, tray in hand with warm tea, a glass of water, toast, and oatmeal. She comes over and sits right on the edge of the couch beside Tygeria, and sets the tray in front of them. She hands Tygeria the glass. Tygeria breathes a sigh of relief and contentment, and slowly she makes her way through eating it all. Pa and Mark plan and talk, then Mark leaves for the night with promises to return in the morning. Ma clears the tray back to the kitchen, and Tygeria falls asleep in the recliner. Pa covers her up with a warm blanket, and then he settles on the couch so he can keep an eye on her.

"My goodness, what she must have been through!" Ma worries.

"Yeah, but she's tough, she will get past this and be all the better for it. She'll just need our help for a while. I'm just so proud of what she did for those people. They said she kept insisting on standing up and blocking anytime someone came in that room. She was determined to defend them even when she had taken quite a beating. We raised one of the good guys, and we raised her tough, now we just need to be patient and helpful, and she will find her way back. I'll work on starting to get her to talk through it."

Recovery is long and hard. She works on walking and getting used to the prosthetic. It's a little hard to balance at first. She keeps walking around the house slow but steady. Building the muscles back and getting to a healthy weight takes time, but they work on it. She can't handle eating anything too rich, so she tries to eat more often. Eventually, she and Ma are taking walks around the edge of the property. It's a three-mile loop if they walk the fence line. She starts taking a hiking stick everywhere she goes. She has a nice one about five feet tall and an inch thick. She starts calling it her staff.

She figures out she can train both the prosthetic and her hiking staff into the energy, it can come and go with the uniform or just by itself. That way, the leg always works, and the stick can be pulled from where she carries it strapped to her back. When she doesn't need it, it is gone but not far. She gets dressed and heads outside.

It's a beautiful morning, only about 70 degrees and the smell of rain in the air. She heads to the barn and uses the open space to start stretching. Then she works on rehearsing the defensive moves she used over and over again in Tzorion's cage, incorporating using the staff into defending herself.

Pa walks in behind her, "You've gotten good."

She stops a minute and stands there, "Had to."

"I know," Pa says, walking over, "does it make you feel safe? In control? Strong?"

She hesitates, thinking, "Yes," She replies.

"But now you're here?" Pa points out, as he walks over to his tool bench. "Do you still need to feel safe? Are you not safe here already?"

Tygeria smiles at him, "Yes, I do." She walks over to him, "But."

"But?" Pa asks.

"When does he come back? When does that happen again? The stronger I am, the less afraid I am, and the more I can handle. I know I'm not about to start kicking the crap out of a human, but I've seen more of what's out there, and all that will find us one day. I will need to handle it. I want to be ready."

"Let's get you comfortable then," Pa says.

He pulls a set of keys out of his workbench and heads over to a locked stall. Inside is a bunch of storage; he goes in and emerges with a punching bag and a chain and hangs it up in the center of the open space where she was training.

"If you want to get stronger, you need something to hit."

He helps her train. She tires quickly for now, and they head in for lunch after a few hours of practice. The days come and go, and she gets stronger, as they keep working.

She is frustrated, "I'm home. I know I'm home," she tells him. "I know I'm safe, but every morning before I am even awake, I'm already…what scared…no not scared. Ready….defensive…not gonna play the victim. OK scared. But it's time for that to stop. There is no one here to kick me awake. No one here to break my ribs. No one here to slice their throat and drag them out."

Pa rushes over and sits beside her on the bed and hugs her, "Hush, it's OK. Take a deep breath. We will get through this."

Tygeria nods and takes a deep breath trying to breathe away the memory of it. At least until the next time she has to wake up.

Pa had packed up all her things at the apartment. Thanks to being gone a year, the gift shop job and the apartment are both gone. Thankfully Pa checked on the apartment and talked with the landlord, in hopes that Tygeria was still alive and would show up again one day he packed everything up and brought it back to her old room at the ranch. Tygeria starts going through the boxes, she doesn't want to unpack too much of it because she needs to find another apartment, but she digs through some of her things trying to find a few essentials.

She rummages through a box, and after deciding everything in there can wait, she seals it back up and opens another. By the third box, she has found her favorite hairbrush and a good pocket knife and set them aside. This box has some books, and a few electronics in it, headphones, power strip, keyboard, speakers, and then she sees it. The guardian cuff. Everything she has been through, she completely forgot about Niemia and the guardian cuff. She slips it on and fills it with energy, and then she seals up that box. Before she can even start the next box, she can feel him outside. His energy is brighter than any living thing around; all guardians are. She stands out the same way to him but doesn't realize it. The doorbell rings.

"I've got it," she says, intercepting Pa. He stops where he is and waits. She opens the door. There is Niemia, and his smile immediately turns to concern because she is still fragile.

"I thought it odd that you seemed to vanish," Niemia says, "something happened, didn't it?"

Tygeria steps outside and invites him to go for a walk. They follow her usual route around the property line. She tells him everything she went through in her time with Tzorion. Carefully she described everything she saw of his compound. She told him she thinks that it is on Sarani, but not sure of that. He takes in every detail.

"Well, there you are," Niemia says, "if you can handle and survive Tzorion, you can certainly help with all the little stuff we deal with every day as guardians. Our attempts to take down the likes of him are few and far between, and those are the toughest things we try. Several of us coming together for those missions makes it far easier, though. It's also worth knowing we have a prison that can hold him; dusting walls won't do him any good where we will put him."

"I think I would like to link to that network of guardians, especially as Central is making plans to explore further and further areas of space." Tygeria says, "I know I want to keep Earth safe, but I don't know what I'm up against. But I don't think I'm gonna be too much help to you now; I haven't even been able to get back to helping with simple fires and crashes here in my own city yet."

"I know you're still getting your strength back. It will come, just keep getting out there," Niemia says, "In the meantime, you might as well meet the other guardians and see how the network works. And don't worry, I've been helping out for some of the big disasters that happened the past year. Partially because I kept knowing I'd find you again that way."

"Nope, you had no hope there, I was not even on the planet," Tygeria says. "But thank you for helping where you could. That's a bit of a relief to hear."

"Well, as you will soon discover when things quiet down on your planet, it's nice to be able to hop over to another planet and find something to help with there," Niemia says.

"So how do I get into this tower?" Tygeria asks him.

They have walked back around to the house, and she heads to the front door.

"The cuff will get you in," Niemia says. Tygeria pokes her head in the front door of the house and lets Pa know she's leaving. Then Niemia shows her how to trigger the cuff while flying up in the air, and then they find themselves popping up through a circle on the floor of the guardian tower. There are screens all around them; the place is the shape of a large cylinder. The screens are showing areas of panic by large masses of people on the surface of the planet. Some of the scenes are riots and protests in other countries on the other side of Earth. Some are images from flooding that is happening on Sarani. Some monitors are black because not enough is happening to trigger them all.

"On a quiet day, it will look like this," Niemia explained, "I checked them just before I came, so I know there isn't any of our kind of thing going on right now."

Niemia walks her around the small circular walkway past the monitors. Your tower right now is just set up for Earth and Sarani. All of the guardians have their own tower, and we are all linked up to more than one planet, but no more than five. There is also no single planet that doesn't have more than one guardian linked. Obviously, we both can watch for alerts on Earth. Your second planet is Sarani, but I can't go directly there unless someone calls for back up because my second planet is Natural. A strange name, but that's what they think of calling a place Earth, pretty strange. I have a third planet, which is good because I won't get to do much on Earth anymore now that you're around."

"So I can't ever get to someone else's tower," Tygeria says, "but I can get to any planet in the network if someone calls for backup?"

"Yes," Niemia pulls what looks like a solid glass ball or sphere out of a pouch hanging from his belt. It is about the size of an orange. When we set these off at a location, it acts as a beacon and automatically links the towers. Any guardian from anywhere can go to their tower and drop down at a sphere location and help out whoever is currently getting their butt kicked." Niemia laughs.

"Well, that's handy," Tygeria says.

"So, what does a busy day look like?" Tygeria asks.

"All these screens will be focused on locations that might need your help, all of them might be scrolling through sites; in fact, five minutes per location and then flipping to the next," Niemia says. "It depends on how much activity there is to show you?"

"Can I use it to see a specific location that I think might have something going on, and just nobody is panicking yet?" Tygeria asks.

"Nope," Niemia says. "That will still require your usual resources, news, Internet, etc. This whole thing is automatic, and your cuff will tingle with energy without you even having to look over at it every time a new alert pops on the screen so you know when you might need to come up here and check—no need to hang out. We are floating in space in high orbit. Environmental controls are making it feel like a building and giving you atmosphere and gravity. All that shuts down when you leave to conserve power, and the sun's UV rays keep everything charged and running."

They select a destination on one of the screens, and the circle on the floor now shows that target as if the tower itself were just floating over that spot on the planet's surface. It's not though it's a transport trick; the view prepares them for where they will emerge, what's going on in real-time, and how much landing room they have.

"Your a flier, so I have it set up for that," Niemia tells her, "it will always drop you up in the air over the scene because that is a huge advantage. Not all guardians can float or fly, so there are ground set transport windows too."

"You can set one permanent location as a home point. Just use this to access the tower from that point, and it will save the location until you change it. You can leave this device here once you set it to what you want."

Niemia shows her a flat card shaped tool. "I brought it up with me when we came just now, so it's set to the ranch."

They each step back onto the center circle that shows the ranch again, and on a timer, they drop into the air space above the ranch and glide down onto the porch.

In a month or two, I will set one of these off," Niemia says, "it will be a location option in your tower. Follow it, and I will gather up a handful of the nearest guardians in the network, and you can meet them."

"I will see you then," Tygeria shakes his hand.

"Glad you're OK," Niemia says, walking away. "I bet, with your experience, we are one step closer to catching Tzorion finally."

Niemia jumps up and transports up to his tower. Tygeria goes back inside and tells Pa that the world just got a whole lot bigger and smaller all at once.

Tygeria decides she is at least strong enough to start patrolling again. She begins by checking back in with her friend. She tells Debbie everything that she went through over the past year. Debbie tells her that she became a bit of a celebrity. Debbie says she kept the blog going even though there were no new rescues to discuss.

The real turning point was when the other 22 survivors that Tzorion held hostage came back and told their stories of what an evil force Tzorion was and how they came to depend on Tygeria's protection. While Niemia took over helping on Earth, he was not afraid of an interview or two. He introduced the concept of the Guardians watching the planets and help-ing. He explained how they already have a guardian, and it's not him. In one interview, when they asked if Tygeria was the Earth's guardian, he said yes, but he fears she might have tried to help them with more than she could handle.

"There was even a movie about it within a few months. Then videos and chats about several of your older rescues kept resurfacing and circulating," Deb-bie says, "You are legendary at this point. I don't think you'll have any more problems with anyone trusting you. We just need to get you back out there."

"Well, I need to get out and glide around," Tygeria says, "I crave that sensation of really circulating that system, and when the weather is nice, it's just invigo-rating."

"Let's see if anything is going on a few states over so you can stretch your wings a bit," Debbie smiles.

"But I don't have wings," Tygeria says.

"Don't get literal on me now," Debbie rolls her eyes, picks up her Ipad, and sits down at the kitchen table to make a few notes.

"I'm gonna head north; just tell me when to turn," Tygeria says. She walks out of the back door and takes off. It's not even dark out yet; she switches to her hero uniform in midair. She has learned to be careful on landings to keep her leg from getting sore. While Debbie checks her usual sources, Tygeria transports into her tower and checks the screens. A lot is going on around the world, but thankfully, not many of them are disasters she can help.

There is a mudslide, she's not even sure of the location, but the tower lets her drop down right over the trouble. She lands ahead of where the mud and dirt and water are flowing and freezes a large part of the front edge. Then she keeps moving one street at a time and fills her staff with energy and slams the tip of it into the mudslide and freezes the slide. Moving quickly, it pauses the destruction long enough for people to get out of the way. There is still a lot of property damage, but in the end, officials decide the slide would have traveled twice as far without intervention.

After the mudslide, she uses the tower to jump back to her city, and Debbie ques her into a runaway semi, then an apartment fire, and after that, a capsized boat off the coast. She handles each one with ease and then calls it a night and heads home worn out and happy.

The headlines the next day shout shes back! Tygeria decides this is the best time to tackle her next big goal. In plain clothes, she catches the train into Earth Central and gets off at the main entrance. She strolls past the souvenir shop where she used to work. She gradually makes her way through the security checkpoint. On the other side, she checks the directory and heads to the Admiral's office on the second floor. When it comes to Earth Central, he is the highest in charge. She walks in to find a receptionist and several uniformed officers waiting in chairs. She can hear the Admiral talking to someone behind the closed door of his office.

"Can I help you?" the receptionist says. "If you saw the sign, this section is for officers only; if you're with the press, you need to go down the hall to the PR office."

"I would like to speak to the Admiral for a few minutes?" Tygeria says, walking over to the receptionist's desk.

"Do you have an appointment?" She asks.

"No, but I think he will want to see me," Tygeria smiles.

She holds her hand over a small piece of paper on the desk, and when she moves it, she has burned her name into the page. She slides it over to the receptionist and then nods. The receptionist's eyes get wide, and she jumps to her feet, looks Tygeria up and down one more time, and then says, one moment, please.

The receptionist knocks on the Admiral's door and enters. Tygeria can hear them talking, and then the receptionist reemerges with three high ranking officers that leave the room looking Tygeria over as they go.

They look confused, probably because she looks so ordinary at this moment.

"This way, please," the receptionist says, holding the door open. The other officers in the room whisper, wondering who this is that just jumped the line ahead of everyone. Tygeria walks into the room.

Admiral Denton is in his mid-40s, quite muscular with dark brown hair, and a very short beard. He has a round face and a slightly tan complexion. There is a scar over his left eyebrow. His desk is very organized and clear of papers except for a few folders that he quickly grabs and sets in a drawer behind him. There is a laptop off to one side of the desk and a phone and notepad on the other. Centered is a high-quality desk plaque reading Admiral Denton. Tygeria's eyes catch a poster on his sidewall that reads, "How far can we go?" and another on a starry outer space background "What arrogance would lead us to think we are the only ones in such a vast universe."

The Admiral also gets a look of confusion on his face, convinced he'd been duped as Tygeria approaches his desk.

"Come on in," Admiral Denton says. "Tygeria, is it? Am I saying that right?"

"Yes," Tygeria says, "my apologies for interrupting, but I thought it was high time for us to meet."

"I agree, but no offense intended you're not quite what I was expecting," the Admiral says as he comes around and leans back against the front of the desk. "How do I know you are who you say you are?"

Tygeria stands about two feet back from him and triggers the energy threads, changing from plain-clothes into her hero uniform, the cloak materializing last, rolling down from her shoulders to the ground.

The Admiral straightens up and stands back a bit as this happens. "Yeah, OK. Wow. I've gotta ask, am I the first formal conversation you've had with some-one, the news reports have had no actual interviews shown."

"Well, I have my network of friends and resources that help me find places I can help and keep me go-ing," Tygeria says.

"Of course," the Admiral says, he shakes her hand, "thank you for all you've done for our city, our coun-try. Actually, I think some reports show you've been all over the world."

"I get around," she smiles. "I'm just one of those people that can't watch trouble without stepping in and helping, granted I can't fix everything but…" Ty-geria says.

"Clearly," the Admiral lets go of her hand and walks back around his desk. "I'm honored to have you here what is it that I can help you with?"

"Actually, I want to help you," Tygeria says, "I've been to Sarani already, and I've tapped into a network of Guardians that have faced all the worst things this program may meet as we join the universal stage. I want us to succeed; hopefully, without making enemies, we don't intend to make. You guys should handle your own politics. I've seen your mission statements you're not planning to conquer or chase resources; you're taking a diplomatic educational approach, and that's good. I think I can help your security team with some good policies and defensive methods that will let you explore without having to kill your way through things nor get yourselves crushed along the way."

"Tempting," the Admiral says. "I wouldn't mind trying you out, see how much you can teach them, and how well they are willing to learn from you."

Tygeria and the Admiral work out an employment arrangement, so she doesn't have to be confined to duties, but she has a rank that commands the respect of officers who don't know her. She works out a modest income so she can still have an off base apartment, and she is flexible to come and go as she needs so she can still patrol and help when needed. Now, however, in her downtime, she can be here helping them not be afraid of new aliens and protecting them from the crazy stuff that might show up through the space dock.

When they finish, he thanks her again for coming, and insists she come back any time there is any way he can help. He gives her papers to get a commander's uniform and get an officer to introduce her to the security team next week. She says she would rather introduce herself if he just wants to give them a heads up that a new commander is coming. He likes that approach and agrees.

Tygeria stood in front of a skeptical group of men and women, all standing at attention in the security team gym room. They are the Earth Central Security team.

It's not Tygeria's style to flash her colors. She doesn't want to come across like she is trying to show off, so she will have to work at it a little to earn the respect of this room.

"It's good to meet you. Your reputation of being an elite security team for Earth's gateway to the Universe has proceeded you." Tygeria addresses a group of 50 officers. "You have kept the officers in line, and as I hear it, you have even thwarted a few sabotage attempts. That's good. It means you have your eyes open. I'm not here to teach you how to be cops for this place. You would not have made it this far if you didn't know how to do that job. What I want to help you with is to make sure you can handle anything that might come through that doorway. Any questions?"

"Request permission to speak freely?" says the center man in the first row.

"Go ahead."

"My name is Reed. I'm your second in command, and I've run this team for two years now. I can't say I have ever heard of you, so I'm curious what it is that you can teach us."

"Let's find out," Tygeria says, hopping down off the platform onto the gym floor. "At ease, guys."

The group stands in place relaxed now but still skeptical.

"You think you can fight me?" Reed smiles.

"I will never strike first, so it depends on what you mean by fight," Tygeria says, "but I wonder if you can take this stone from my hand?"

She pulls a stone out of her pocket and holds it out palm up to show him, then she closes her hand and stands arms at her side in a casual but alert stance, feet apart.

"OK, " Reed replies.

He lunges at her hand, but she casually dodges. So he tries to grab her by the other arm, but she ducks, spins, and stands behind him before he knows whats happened. They continue a fast-paced almost dance, and then Tygeria sweeps Reed's legs out from under him and lands him on his back.

"OK, so your quick, that is pretty impressive," Reed says, getting to his feet again. "But what's the story the guys tell, when a 20-foot beast bursts through that door, how are you going to take care of it?"

"Well, I've thrown a grown man across the room into the wall before," she replies, "so I'm sure I would toss the beast back through the door. But I want to get you guys the right plan so that you don't need me to do that."

"Permission to speak freely?" the Sanarian Cirk says from the line.

"Granted," Tygeria walks toward him.

"What is your name, chief?" Cirk said it with hesitation like he's asking something that sounds like he shouldn't. He just wanted the rest of the room to know. I suppose he was trying to make it easier on her.

"Tygeria," she replied.

Cirk gets the gasp from the room that he wanted. The whole room stands up a little straighter. "You are Earth's Guardian, aren't you?"

"I've been called that yes," Tygeria says. "Chief will work for you guys; I'm just here to help. Reed, can you return them to their activities, then we should talk a minute."

"Aye Chief," Reed replies.

He orders the teams back to their various assignments. "We have an office over here," he offers, and Tygeria and Reed go talk for a bit. They chat for a while, just getting to know each other.

"So let me ask you," Tygeria changes the topic, "What are you afraid of for this place."

"Pretty much what you said," Reed answers, "something coming through that space dock door that just swats us like flies or something."

"Well, I'm relieved to discover that the barrier around Central is going to keep anything from wrecking the world, but Central is still vulnerable for a good stomping," Tygeria says.

"What can I do for you?" Reed says.

The excitement comes through in his voice. The potential of how good this team can get is starting to sink in.

"Two ideas. First, I want you to pick your best fighter, and your best tactical person and the four of us will meet Monday, I will start letting you know some of the stuff I've run into when I go through the tower and help on other planets. And we can play what if it comes through the door what we would do. You guys can help me figure out the best way to get that group to handle it as a team. That leads me to the other idea. I think we need a team of ten elite security officers that are going to take the lead on handling the crazy stuff. Don't pull them from the rotations. Everyone still needs to take their turns walking the halls, but only those ten will do the extra training and will need to respond to alarms set off from all the people coming in with deliveries for the big meeting with the Sanarians."

"Sounds good to me, I'll set both those up while you work on getting us our overrides," Reed says. "So nobody else here realizes who you are, I mean the Admiral does that's clearly why he hired you into this position."

"Yes, he's the only other one," Tygeria replies. "I'm going to go enjoy that anonymity while it lasts and walk the grounds and halls, get to know the place, and figure out my routes."

"Don't you think the press should know you are leading security, I bet it would put a lot of people at ease. No one is going to recognize you in a security uniform, even if it is head of security," Reed says.

"I'm sure I'll be jumping off the walls soon enough, and then they'll figure it out," Tygeria replies. "I'm not going to try to hide that I'm Tygeria, but I'm not going to go out there flaunting it either, it's just not my style."

"OK," Reed says. "Can I tell them?"

"Sure, but they won't believe you," Tygeria laughs.

Then she stands and gives him a firm handshake. "I have a feeling we're going to make a good team Reed."

She leaves the office, crosses the gym, and heads out to walk the halls of the massive complex.

Sure enough, the headlines the next day says Tygeria new head of security at Earth Central leading into the big meeting with the Sanarians.

Episode 10

"The way to best serve the interests of Earth Central as we meet new species is to take a defensive approach when it comes to security," Tygeria says.

She is in the gym, surrounded by ten officers from the security team.

"I don't know about you, but if I step up to a bully, the best thing I can do is be the stronger, faster, tougher one." One of the officers says.

"React from fear?" Tygeria asks him.

"I suppose it's certainly better than being killed." The officer points out.

"How menacing is it to step up to someone who just stands there but manages to duck every strike and not be emotionally phased one bit. Does their opponent not feel like a failure in that scenario." Tygeria says.

"I see the value in acting like every fight is beneath us, but when they strike out, we can't always duck every strike they try." The officer points out.

"Why not? If it's important to you, you certainly can be quick, be confident, be strong-willed, and we will be safe out there." Tygeria says.

They start working on defensive moves with staffs, blocking, and disarming opponents, ducking and dodging becomes the dance of the training floor. They drill by practicing on each other over and over.

Reed and Tygeria are walking the corridors of Earth Central and pop into the large meeting room where the meeting will happen between Humans and Sanarians.

"The main program the Captains had me teaching all the security officers was a numbers game, making sure you outnumber and can overpower the other side just in case the conversations when meeting new people go wrong. I like your approach better. The officers and security will still feel safe, and so should the people we meet not feel threatened. I like it."

"There are two main motivators in life, fear and greed. How we let them influence our decisions says a lot about our character. I know how Tzorion handles fear; he uses oppression and control to manage others, so he does not have to be afraid of them. Nor afraid of his medical condition. This terrorist group handles their fear of cooperating with the Sanarians through destruction and trying to make others afraid." Tygeria says.

"What was one of the first questions I asked you, Reed?" Tygeria says.

"Actually, after you asked me where I was from and stuff, I remember you asked me what I was afraid of," Reed says.

"I believe that the best defense to fear is knowledge," Tygeria says. "The more the public understands about how alike humans and Sanarians are, the more relaxed and less fearful they will be. These terrorists will stop getting any support."

"It's my understanding that we have learned a lot about them through all the conversations the outreach team has had. Can we start publicizing some of that leading up to their arrival? We need to get the general public excited for our first actual contact," Tygeria says.

The cross is a large meeting room. It sits 400 people in bleacher sections around the edges. The flat floor in the middle has been set up with tables to seat just as many 400. There is a stage at the front with three large screens on the wall behind it. Centered on the stage is a podium. The whole room has a color scheme of dark green, navy blue, and gold.

Thacher is in the meeting room at the terrorist office downtown. The table is crowded with an angry bunch. They are upset that nothing has managed to cancel the planned arrival of the Sanarians. Earth Central decided they will throw a big banquet, food, and discussion about how the two civilizations can best coexist.

"We have one week left before their banquet," Thacher says, "at this point, our only move left to stop this nonsense seems to be to make the Sanarians afraid of Humans. We must sabotage the banquet with as much chaos as we can muster. We are going to set fire in the banquet room, and we are planting a bomb on the train, which will take out three buildings if set off in the right location. Does everybody know their part?"

They all agree, in one week, they will execute the next strike. They will meet up three days after the attack to discuss the results and plan the future. They all file out of the office and lock it tight.

Back at Earth Central, Tygeria and Reed are walking through the courtyard past the medical building and research building toward the food court. It is a rainy day. They stroll under the awnings to keep cover from the rain. Officers and delivery men are hurriedly crossing the courtyard. The rain has been falling steadily all day.

Tygeria and Reed are discussing the extra security that might be needed for the arrival of the Sanarians. "Everyone inside Central will have to go through the scanners, so I'm not worried about any weapons or explosives inside that way. It's the space doc and the transportation perimeter we have to worry about," Tygeria says.

"So that's the parking garage though that's a bit far away, the fields and that delivery road," Reed says.

"What sort of security do the deliveries pass through?" Tygeria asks.

"We don't scan the trucks, just the workers, and their loads as they come into the actual property with each cart full," Reed explains.

"Of course, there is also the train. Those stations are around the city, so we can't set security at all of those." Tygeria says.

"Passengers are screened right after they come off, that will catch anything there," Reed says.

"I think the delivery trucks would be where the terrorists would try something." Tygeria decides.

One of Tygeria's security officers comes to the office door and knocks, then opens the door. "So sorry to interrupt Tygeria, but the Admiral is asking for you. He is in his office."

"OK, thank you," Tygeria says.

"I guess I'd better see what he needs," Tygeria says.

"I'll start looking at our options for the delivery trucks." Reed says, "I might just look for a station we can set up by the road where we can stop them and use some bomb-sniffing dogs."

Tygeria heads out of the Security Office, across the training gym and the main courtyard to the offices. She takes the elevator up and leads to the Admirals office. This time she is dressed like any other security officer in the building except for the cords on her shoulder, showing that she is in leadership. She walks through the Admiral's outer office to the receptionist. She remembers this time and stands up right away.

"This way, please," the receptionist says as she heads straight to the Admiral's door and opens it for her.

"Tygeria, please come on in," Admiral Denton says. "How are things going for you?"

Admiral Denton is standing in front of his chair behind his desk. She walks to one of the chairs in front of his desk and takes a seat. The Admiral is an officer and a gentleman, so he waits until Tygeria sits then he sits back in his chair. "Thank you for coming. I hope I didn't interrupt anything important."

"We are preparing for the banquet Admiral, not much to do but plenty to worry about," Tygeria says.

"I am glad we have you," Admiral Denton says. "From what Reed tells me, you have a robust diplomatic approach to security that is a refreshing change. I have all faith that the meeting with the Sanarians will go smoothly."

"Thank you, Admiral, the position was everything I've been hoping for." Tygeria says, "so what is it I can help you with?"

"I was hoping you would join us." Admiral Denton says. "You are half Human and half Sanarian. You already have the respect of most of the officers in the room. We will be announcing the three Captains of the ships. I would like to have you there and formally announce your position here to the world. I know the Sanarians also have bioenergy like you. A much smaller amount, nothing they can manipulate like you, but the researchers tell me they can recognize each other with their eyes closed because of it. I imagine you will be recognized as one of them right away. Someone linked to both sides like that sure would help the negotiations."

"Can I ask," Tygeria says, "what are you hoping to negotiate. Or is this just a get to know diner?"

"I think I'm hoping to make it mostly a get to know each other diner, but the long-distance conversations have let us get to know quite a bit of each others view on exploring the universe," Admiral Denton says."According to them, they have little cruiser ships but not near the capacity to build large explorer ships like we have. They would actually like to join our program and explore with us side by side with our officers. They say that in exchange, they will share their universal translators, the technology for access windows, which sounds something like a transporter from the ground to ship, and their start charts. Their charts don't go far because their ships don't go far, so they are looking to be a part of going farther."

"To answer your question, I want to go farther, safely, and they are a few decades ahead of us on interacting with the universe beyond their planet. I will feel safer with them along and the bits of technology they offer. Everything we can learn how to do them better," Admiral Denton says.

"OK, I'll come," Tygeria says. "I will arrive late. I need time to make sure the event is secure."

"Of course," Admiral Denton says as he stands up. "You should always feel free to follow your protective instincts above all else. I would have it no other way."

Thacher is at the downtown train station waiting for the next train to arrive. He checks his watch as it pulls up. He stands, steps onto the train, and takes a window seat near the front. He spends the next two hours riding the entire loop until it stops. The medical district stop, state fair park station, the station for the large remote parking, Earth Central station, then the cultural district, the big museum, the airport, and the downtown station, then it goes around again. Thacher gets back off at the same stop he started at downtown.

"Reed," Tygeria calls as she enters the security gym.

Some of the officers are training, and others are patrolling the campus, checking all the busyness.

"Yes, Commander."

Reed crosses the room with a quick but steady step. "We need to make it known that there will be no deliveries on the day of the big meeting. Everything needed must arrive before, and anything not needed can wait until after. Would you put someone on it, have them put a sign up at the delivery gate?"

"Yes commander," Reed says, then he leaves to take care of it.

"For your approval," Lieutenant Brook announces as he comes over.

He is a tall man. Not only is he one of the members of Central Security, but he is also on Tygeria's elite team of ten training to be the first responders to any unique emergencies, whatever may arise.

"What is this for, why are we changing the trains this close to the big event?" Tygeria asks him as kindly as possible.

"Many of the leaders coming from the United Nations are complaining that they cannot be dropped off by their cars, and the compromise is that if everyone must ride the train that we make a special car and schedule everyone for their specific turn. We have sorted all of that out, but these are the changes to the actual car to formal it up a bit," Officer Brook explains.

"I see," Tygeria says. "Well, that is understandable."

She looks over the plans, and it is all decorative changes, so she sees no trouble with it.

"When the changes are done, let me check the actual train cars before we put them in service, even if it has to be early that morning."

Tygeria heads head home for the night after that. Pa is sitting in his recliner in the ranch house watching the evening news on TV. It's mid-week now. A news report breaks the reporter Ted Wiley comes on TV, "As Earth Central prepares for the big day this Saturday the local hotels are filling with some celebrity guests for the event. Several dignitaries from around the world will be attending as the leaders of Earth Central, and the Sanarians work out what their new working relationship will look like. In related news, the guardian angel of the city of Worth has turned up a new position. Tygeria has joined Earth Central and is Head of Security. She will lead, train, and help with security concerns as they open the spaceport to travelers. It's been said that this will not interfere with her usual heroic activities. She apparently has joined a group that lets her travel quickly and freely to many worlds, and now Earth Central will benefit from that experience as well."

"Well, there she is," Pa says to Ma, "she found her niche after all."

"She is going to wear herself out," Ma says.

Pa smiles, "She'll be so happily exhausted, though."

Tygeria arrives at the office in the security room, not a place where she spends much time, but she wants to make sure she has covered everything. After about ten minutes, Brook enters the office, "My apologies commander, but the VIP car on the train is ready for inspection. We wanted to have it done early."

"I'll be right there."

She checks the VIP car or the train, and they put it into service, restricted use by appointment only.

The Earth Central Campus has a large hotel on the west side to house all the visitors. The visiting Sanarians are staying on their ships. As the visitors arrive a few days early, they walk through the security checks and then check-in at the hotel. Tygeria paces the campus nervously. She is nervous about keeping anything from happening though she is convinced the terrorist group will not miss this opportunity to strike. She is excited to meet people from another world and compare their space programs, hopefully merging them. She is nervous about having the Sanarians see her, will they be accepting of her or will they think of her as a muddled up disgrace, a freak born of two types of blood. So she paces around the halls patrolling.

With all the excitement of the week, she has noticed a few more people and officers both glancing her way and smiling. She forgot for a moment that now the world knows who she is, even without her cloak showing. There is no more hiding now. Hopefully, that works out OK, but as she walks around and greets some of the shop and office workers on the perimeter of the campus, she can tell they are glad she's here. The week is less scary for them.

Thursday night Tygeria pops up to the guardian tower and checks it, the screens only focus on all the gatherings around the world where viewing parties have been set up. Starting tonight, they are showing documentaries about the building of Earth Central and the construction of the ships. The whole two-year history of the program has been well documented, and it is playing as viewing parties gather up until the moment of the live broadcast of the banquet. At the dinner, they will announce and decorate the new Captains and officially release the ship assignments, so the officers all know what crew they will have. Then the top ten leaders of Earth Central and the top ten leaders of the Sanarian space program will go to sit in another room and discuss how they might help each other.

Friday afternoon, the campus has calmed down. Everything is in place in the auditorium, so Tygeria and Reed head to check. Tygeria changes into her cloak and pulls her staff from its sash on her back. She fills the staff with energy and taps the end of in into the blue velvet carpet on the auditorium floor. The energy spreads like a ripple through the entire room as she checks for anything that might be harmful. All the universal translator earpieces are in place; the formal diner wear is set, floral centerpieces are filled. Tygeria's energy helps her spot some electronics up at the podium in separate boxes. She walks that way to check them out.

"The room seems fine," Tygeria says to Reed, who is following one step behind, "there is just something up here I need a closer look at."

She steps up onto the stage and opens one of the boxes with the Captain's rank bands in them. The band is beautifully displayed in the box. The band itself will fasten on their shoulder on their uniform to signify they are a captain. Odd that anything electrical is under it. She removes the mounting from the box and exposes a rigged flare underneath it, set to be set off by timer.

"Wow, that's no good," Reed says, alarmed that they found a weapon.

They go through all three, set the mounted bands back on the podium without their box, and take the boxes back to the security office. Behind the training gym are two lab areas run by science officers for investigating and fingerprinting and collecting evidence. Earth Central wants to handle all of its investigations. In that lab, there is a large steel box reinforced with the same technology that creates the protective energy dome around earth central. They place the devices in there and ask the lab to find and note anything they can.

"Glad you caught that," Reed says, "I'll inform the Admiral.

"Go ahead," Tygeria says, "I'll check the room one more time, and then I'm going to lock it up until tomorrow afternoon. Short of a fistfight, we should be OK tomorrow."

"I believe we will," Reed says.

Saturday morning arrives, and Tygeria starts the day at the train station at Earth Central. The train pauses, and the passengers are asked to get off for twenty minutes. Most of them head into the Central Food Court to grab coffee and snacks. Then Tygeria, Reed, and her Elite security team start walking and inspecting the train.

Tygeria puts her hand against the wall of the VIP car and scans the entire train from there within five minutes. She finds nothing threatening, but she likes her team to finish looking as well, so she leaves them to it. When they finish, security steps off, and they let the passengers back on. That train takes on an abridged route, and another one runs the rest of the loop for the day. The second train will never come past central that day, only this one. For today it is a broken loop with turn arounds at the ends instead. The VIP train does go by the parking for the officers and back to Earth Central.

The Admiral has asked that Tygeria stand at the main auditorium entrance with him as all the guests file in, only to leave if something comes up. Everything is running smoothly, so she plans on joining him.

The city is alive with excitement. Music plays, inside and outside dining is filled, and watch parties ramp up. The roads are only lightly traveled, everyone is making a day of it, and most have already arrived wherever they plan on celebrating. Afternoon approaches more quickly than anyone expects.

Thacher parks a car at the off-site parking. He gets out and carefully removes a heavy rolling crate from the trunk. He extends it's pulling handle and closes the trunk. Then he pulls the enclosed crate along behind him and heads up to catch the train. It is making a short run, Thacher takes a window seat near the front with his crate at his feet, and he remains there as the train comes and goes on its short route. He reads a book hoping to be ignored.

The Sanarians are at the Space Dock, and a large group of them starts to make their way off the ships. They open a transport window to a pre-agreed upon location in the courtyard across from the banquet hall. Everyone is in place, and the guests all start arriving. Humans are entering the auditoriums from the side doors off of the trains, presenting their IDs for admission. The lists get checked, and only those on the list get in. It is a long list. Several of those that come off the trains end up setting off the security arches. Most of them check their guns and knives at a station set up for that purpose. In all, 13 people are escorted away by security for trying to bring weapons into the event.

The Sanarians arrive through the transport window, walking in clusters of two and three. Sanarians turn out to look just like any human for the most part. Just like Tygeria, most of the differences are on the inside, and they are subtle at that. These Sanarian explorers that have come are all wearing their own kind of uniform. There are both men and women present. They are all in a short sleeve, pantsuit with a decorative sash, and signifies rank. The sash is fastened tight with a belt at the waist. None of them are armed with any weapons, of course, and most are wearing universal translators in their ear. Tygeria's security team and the admiral are wearing them as well.

"Welcome to Earth," the Admiral says as the first Sanarian officers approach.

"Thank you, what an exciting place you have set up here," the lead Sanarian says. "And you," he offers his hand to Tygeria and gives a firm handshake. "You are our lost daughter of Sarani we have heard about. You have done good things, I understand."

"It's a pleasure to meet you. I'm glad the two space programs will be working together," Tygeria says.

"Indeed," he says, then he continues into the auditorium.

The others follow, they chat less with the humans, but they talk a little with each other, mainly just noting their surroundings. Clearly, they are excited.

The banquet eventually gets started after all the hundreds attending settle in. Tygeria's nerves settle quite a bit; everything is off to a good start; she wants to patrol the area to make sure it stays that way. The Admiral excuses himself and heads for the banquet stage to greet all his guests and tell them to insert their universal translators in their ears. He goes through an elaborate greeting painting a bright future for the future of both planets, which is well received. Then he calls up the new Captains who will head theses new ships that will leave next week and presents them with their Captain bands very ceremoniously. Then he invites all to eat and visit and enjoy. There will be further negations that evening between those who will be managing the ships and the merger.

Thacher is still on the train watching the broadcast on his phone. As they break to dine, he flips a switch in the case, pulls a device out of his pocket, and stands up as they approach the next train stop. Thacher steps off the train onto the platform at the parking station. He fiddles with the device, which ends up being a detonator, just to make sure it is getting a good signal. The train pulls away, heading back to Earth Central Station. He starts counting out as he has been over and over again, timed to the exact count that the train will arrive at Earth Central Station.

Reed steps up behind Thacher on the platform, and two other security officers come from different directions.

"Come with me, please," Reed insists.

Hurriedly, Thacher presses the button, nothing.

Tygeria is on the train. The officer trailing Thacher is standing in the aisle as Tygeria pulls the crate into the aisle. It has been unplugged and frozen solid for good measure. They take a few quick pictures of the device as the train pulls into the station. When the doors open, faster than can be seen, Tygeria shoots up into the air with the package and throws it into space well away from the space station. It never explodes, but they didn't want to take any chances.

The train stops running for a few hours to be re-checked; then, it resumes its route for the day. There are a few passengers since the big event has started already.

Tygeria gets to attend the meeting. It is decided that some Sanarian officers will be allowed into the university to train as officers and join the ships. A few will be fast-tracked due to current experience and will join the maiden voyages. In exchange for letting their people come along, they will share some of their technology, transport windows, translators, and some of the medical advances that can likely be converted to help humans as well. Everyone is excited as the night wraps up.

Admiral Denton pulls Tygeria aside at the end of it all, "I have already heard about several thwarted attempts to disrupt this great day, I owe you my thanks. Job well done."

"I'm glad it has all gone so well," Tygeria says.

"What do you think?" admiral Denton asks her, "can we trust them?"

"I imagine they are asking the same thing about us," Tygeria says. "I think every culture has those with good intentions and bad. We can either avoid all of it, the brilliant and the greedy, or we can take it one situation at a time. I am starting to learn that the latter is pretty much the only way to go. Trouble cannot be fully predicted nor avoided; we just need to be ready to handle it best we can if trouble finds us, and enjoy the brilliant adventure in between."

"I fully agree with that," Admiral Denton says as they walk out from the auditorium. "We are walking into an exciting future even if it may be dangerous."

"I'm always happy to step out first, Admiral."

Tygeria smiles.

www.ingramcontent.com/pod-product-compliance
Lightning Source LLC
Chambersburg PA
CBHW070309040726
47501CB00018B/1360